"TOPPING OUT"

2ND EDITION

KATHERINE WONN HARRIS

BALBOA
PRESS

A DIVISION OF HAY HOUSE

Balboa Press books may be ordered through booksellers or by contacting:

Balboa Press
A Division of Hay House
1663 Liberty Drive
Bloomington, IN 47403
www.balboapress.com
1 (877) 407-4847

Because of the dynamic nature of the Internet, any web addresses or
links contained in this book may have changed since publication and
may no longer be valid. The views expressed in this work are solely those
of the author and do not necessarily reflect the views of the publisher,
and the publisher hereby disclaims any responsibility for them.

The author of this book does not dispense medical advice or prescribe the use
of any technique as a form of treatment for physical, emotional, or medical
problems without the advice of a physician, either directly or indirectly. The
intent of the author is only to offer information of a general nature to help
you in your quest for emotional and spiritual well-being. In the event you use
any of the information in this book for yourself, which is your constitutional
right, the author and the publisher assume no responsibility for your actions.

Print information available on the last page.

ISBN: 978-1-5043-9564-9 (sc)
ISBN: 978-1-5043-9565-6 (hc)
ISBN: 978-1-5043-9596-0 (e)

Library of Congress Control Number: 2018900722

Balboa Press rev. date: 04/13/2018

Contents

Preface

My aunt, Katherine Wonn Harris was a one of a kind person. Besides teaching school in the wild Salmon/Snake River country of Idaho, Katherine was a County Schools Superintendent in Curry County, Oregon. Her dog carried her books. After WWII, Katherine worked as a newspaper woman and found her final home in a small town in Lebanon, Oregon, where she was a feature writer for the "Lebanon Express". Her often humorous stories included people and animals. Her empathy for people and animals is shown in her novel. When she was 70, she published her autobiographical novel, after making a couple of trips back to the Snake and Salmon River country of Idaho where she had been the young "school ma'am". Katherine had a deep appreciation for the waters of the Salmon and Snake Rivers so she included background material in her novel about the "waters". She also felt empathy for the pack horses and wrote a chapter about them. Katherine's colorful writing leads you from page to page so that your senses and emotions are truly satisfied.

My vision for this editing and republishing of this book is to make the book accessible to everyone from age 10-100, especially to high school girls in both the United States, Canada and Mexico. It is an adventure story. Anyone who values places of nature, loves people and animals will love this book.

The original charming drawings by Bonnie D. Joseph, granddaughter of Chief Joseph make the book come alive.

The book was first copyrighted in 1971 by Katherine's friend, Aldyth Logan of Idaho. Katherine passed this life in 1979 and her novel was bequeathed to me, as a "kindred spirit". She drew the Idaho Map. – Marilyn Allen, "Publisher, 2nd Edition".

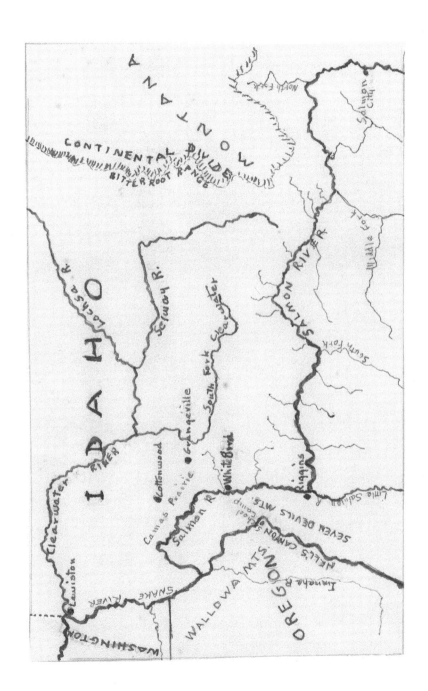

Acknowledgements

Thanks to Balboa Press editor, Holly S. Thank you to my step-son, Jay, my husband, Chuck and of course, all of the people who made the book possible. May this beautiful writing live forever.

Photo of illustrator, author and original publisher circa 1971
(Bonnie D. Joseph, Katherine Wonn Harris, Aldyth Logan)

Prologue

A pattern of life that had prevailed for a half a century was approaching its end in 1916 when I first came to the lower Salmon River country. A large part of its people made up a nomadic society, and they were the well-to-do who controlled enormous range acreages and counted their cattle by the thousands. They moved with their herds as the seasons dictated, but they were most truly at home on the river where their cattle winter-ranged.

Here was the home ranch, general headquarters, and core of their enterprise. What meager conveniences they had—their best home furnishings and their most substantial buildings, were centered here. An irrigation system, which tapped a creek high in its canyon and led water by ditches and flumes down harsh draws and around mountainsides to their hay fields, frequently cost more than all their other improvements.

Their second home was generally known as the "upper place." It commanded the area of spring and fall range. When cattle topped out for summer range in the high country, they moved on to their third home, the summer camp.

After the fall roundup, when cattle were cut out and the

long drive to a distant railroad terminal began, the families marshaled their pack outfits and, with their remaining herds, moved down the mountain to the upper place, where they lived while stock spread out on the fall range. As frost crept lower, the cattle were gradually drifted to the home range, and the fourth move of the year took the family back to their river ranch, still languorous in Indian summer, gardens still in late bearing, and the orchards heavy with fruit.

Snow lay deep on the summer camps and dusted the upper place, but winter touched the canyon bed lightly. The period of feeding was usually short, and this season afforded the stockman the nearest to leisure he could know. He fed his weaker cattle, rode the low range to check the stock wintering out, made repairs on riding and packing equipment, and planned a year ahead for his necessities.

Spring bursts on the river with lusty exuberance, intense with color and sound and odor. Melting snows all over the vast altitudes that spawn the river's feeders send down contributions. The Salmon becomes swollen and horrible. It is brown—the color of earth; it is the bleeding of a vast hinterland. A monstrous crest forms in its middle and great trees are tossed about like sticks. The gigantic boulders on its bed are rolled and beaten, and their crashing fills the canyon with dull thunder.

This was a time of intense activity on the river ranches. Saddle and packhorses were rounded up and brought in for shoeing. Gardens were planted, hay fields seeded, ditches and flumes repaired, drift fences put in shape, cattle gathered from winter range, and final preparations made for the movement up the mountain.

In this fluid manner, life went on for more than fifty years. It is now history, though the country itself has not changed. Its harshness has not softened, but the world around it has.

Many reasons have been given for the epoch's end. Some say that the terrible winter of 1920 dealt the stockmen a blow from which they never recovered. Few forgot it, for the Salmon was so deeply frozen that cattle could be crossed on the ice, and heavy snow blanketed the entire area. Caught with inadequate feed, trapped in the canyon with their starving herds, the ranchers suffered crushing losses.

Others claim that the cycle was broken by the noxious goat weed that moved in from the Clearwater country, attacking spring and fall range and almost totally destroying it.

Doubtless the whole system was doomed when the American public began to demand small cuts of beef, tender, thick morsels from fat, young animals. Lusty slabs from a four-year-old steer were not styled to new America's tastes. This meant a new type of feeding and a finishing process entirely alien to the old range cycle.

I contend that women contributed in some measure to the end of nomadic existence. A few accepted and managed their place in it, but the majority hated it and warred ceaselessly against it. It was all very well for the men—the risks, the excitement, the ever-present dangers of managing half-wild animals on precipitous trails, the annual gamble of insufficient feed against a possible hard winter, the pitting of skill and courage against the harshest of lands.

But for the women, it meant uprooting an entire household

four times a year. It meant hungry hordes to feed, for every outfit had its hired men and an assortment of hangers-on. It meant men riding in at all hours to be fed and bedded. It meant no schools beyond the elementary grades in the one-room school, no church, no social life, the constant menace of the river, and the feeling of never being settled. All contributed to a vast discontent. It was endurable when the West's entire society was on a frontier basis, but when life outside took on leisure and refinement, when labor-saving devices entered the home, the women of the Salmon River compared their brutal surroundings with the advantages of their sisters outside, and their protests increased.

As I frequently joined in these protests myself, it is hard to say why I continued to go back to the country for seven years, teaching in its river schools, mining camps, and short-term summer schools and tutoring where public school was not possible. I was often asked, "Why are you wasting your young life in this country when you could be teaching in a modern city school?"

Perhaps I clung too long to values that slipped rapidly from our entire world after 1914. These changes came very slowly to the canyon country, and in many of its sections they are not apparent to this day. Nor was I satisfied there, for I felt out of the stream of life and was filled with a vague longing to join my roaring generation as it rushed forward to embrace new days and new ways. But when I left between school terms, vowing never to return, I was soon bewildered in the towns and cities of a changing society. My old school friends were scattered, and those left were estranged by glittering new goals to which I attached little value.

Depressed in spirit, I longed for the peace and deep security of the canyons. Lonely and without direction, unable to resolve my conflicts, I fled back to the river to reestablish myself again with the life and people dear to me through familiarity and tradition.

It was a rough life with no refinements. Everything was done the hard way, for there was no other means, but my years there were not wasted. What progress I have made toward being a person, the measure of maturity I have been able to achieve, has deep roots in that country. Its people, without pretense and real as the rock of their canyons, will forever live in my memory with deep tenderness and thanksgiving that the human spirit can be so tough.

1

Down to the Salmon

"There she lays," the stage driver said as he pointed. "Yonder's a big hunk of the Salmon River country."

The panorama suddenly revealed from the rim of Idaho's high Camas Prairie was a fantasy in dimensions. I gazed out over the nation's greatest continuous expanse of blue peaks and rugged gorges, many unexplored. Here, within a fifty-mile radius, lay the three deepest river canyons on the continent—Hells Canyon of the Snake, the Salmon River Gorge, and that of its Middle Fork.

From ridge to ridge, the immensity rose and fell into the mist of its own purple horizon. Out to our right, grand in its dusky depth, one predominant chasm coiled into the tapestry of distance.

"That's part of the lower Salmon gorge." The driver followed its sweep of fantastic color and distance with a wide gesture.

"I had no idea it was so wide! So deep!" I exclaimed.

"This don't hold a candle to the upper Salmon country," he explained. "Don't suppose you'll ever see it though. Most schoolma'ams get mighty river shy after the first year, especially if they come from the city, and I'd guess you do." His glance flicked over my velvet toque; tailored tricotine suit and high-heeled, buttoned shoes.

"My folks live in Boise," I said.

"I'd guess this is your first school too," he announced.

Uneasily I admitted this, wondering if, in spite of my grown-up lady's costume, I looked as young as my sixteen years. I wanted desperately to look eighteen, the minimum age required by Idaho for teaching. Feeling guilt for the false statements made to the examining board and in various applications for schools, I wanted no discussion on the subject of age.

He spoke some more. "And I'd guess again that you don't know much about this country, or you'd have left that trunk at home. A big box thing like that can cause a sight of misery traveling like you'll have to do from now on."

I didn't like my shiny new trunk called "a big box thing," but I had to admit that it had already caused considerable trouble, for in order to load it that morning, the rear stage seat had to be removed. Fortunately, I was the only passenger for the canyon country. I glanced back at my treasure surrounded by mailbags and sundry freight items. Already its glossy surface was coated with dust.

"I wouldn't have brought it if I'd come straight through

by stage from Boise," I apologized. "But they said part of the road was out from a cloud burst, and I couldn't get to White Bird that way. Had to come by train around through Oregon and Washington to Lewiston and take that jerkwater line up to Grangeville. Just think—three days to get a hundred miles from home."

"Just as well, though," remarked the driver. "That stage road north from Boise is a heller at best. Takes as long, too, with stopovers and all, and you'd have been plenty shook up."

"The ticket agent thought I'd get almost to White Bird on the train. It looked such a little way from Grangeville on the map."

"A little way on a map don't mean a thing in this country," the driver commented grimly.

After a tug on the reins, the team moved along the narrow road on the edge of the prairie. In spite of my wretched night spent in Grangeville, I took a last long look back to its faint smudge on the horizon. It was to be my last contact with life's easier ways for a longer time than I then knew. In that raw frontier town, built by cattle, mines, and wheat, I had spent my first night of total aloneness and my first sojourn ever in a hotel. Booted feet had clumped up and down the hall, accompanied by loud laughter and profanity. There had been raucous whoops in the street, and at intervals horses were ridden up and down the boardwalks. When midnight passed and the tempo increased, I arose, dressed, and sat on the bed until dawn brought a lull in the merriment.

When I went downstairs for an early breakfast, the desk

clerk apologized for the uproar. "The boys like to celebrate a little on Saturday nights," he explained.

The edge of the prairie was close. The road dipped to the rim, and we started over.

Far below, our way wound steadily downward. Several switchbacks were already in sight. It seemed a desperate descent to the bottom of the vast declivity. I set my feet and took a firm grip on the seat. The rangy bay team upped their rumps against the downward push of the surrey; the driver's foot pushed gently and then harder on the brake. Iron tires screeched on wooden brake blocks, and a cascade of dust rose with each wheel turn, encasing us in a smothering cloud.

"This here's a twelve-mile grade, and she's down every foot of the way," said my companion. "But there's no need to be nervous. I drive it every day."

The vast panorama was snatched from us as we clattered down the grade. Rapidly we sank into the mass of steep, brown hills. Gigantic outcrops of lava towered above us, and the road twisted between massive boulders. My trunk worked loose from its moorings and shifted forward against the seat, threatening to catapult us over the dashboard.

At the next switchback, we halted. The driver set the brakes, handed me the reins, and alighted to chock the wheels. Then he set about the task of arresting the movement of my roving luggage, pushing it back, and using additional rope to anchor it. Acutely embarrassed, I gripped the reins tensely and considered the "sight of misery" my box thing had already caused.

Down we went and still down. The sere grasses of the upper level gave way to sturdier stands of milkweed and thistle. Chokecherry bushes began to appear, their leaves and fruit heavy with dust. Occasionally, we spanned a gully between hills where a brave trickle of water greened the weeds and grass along its course.

There was no tenseness in my driver's leather brown face. His eyes squinted against the billowing dust, and he slouched at ease against the low seat back. Only the grip of his hands on the reins and the forward thrust of his foot against the brake showed constant vigilance. I began to relax.

"How big a town is White Bird?" I asked.

"Not very big," he said. "Couple of stores, bunch of saloons, bank, and hotel."

"I hope someone's there to meet me."

"There will be," he said. "Never no question but some of the young bucks around will be there to meet the new schoolma'am. They just fight for the chance."

I could feel a flush creep up under the coat of dust that covered my face. "I'm not teaching the town school, you know. It's at Buck Creek. Do you know where it is?"

"Sure, I know!" he exclaimed with sudden interest. "It's across the river up between the forks of the Salmon and the Snake. Pretty country up there, but rough."

"Rougher than this?" I asked quickly.

"Well, yes, ma'am, it's considerable steep country. But," he added, "there's a wagon road in there for a piece. You can always get out. Where you going to stay?"

"With one of the school directors. He wrote me about it. His name is Sanson. Know him?"

"Sure do. Jess Sanson's an old-timer in these parts. Got a little ranch, thousand acres or so, about six miles up from the river. Most of that country in there is run by two big cattle outfits, but Sanson has managed to hold on. They're nice folks. You'll like 'em. And," he added silkily, "they've got a nice young son, good-looking kid. Rides for the Wynn outfit when he isn't working for his old man's place. Wouldn't wonder if he'd be in White Bird to meet you."

The warm September sun beat down on the topless surrey endlessly, the wheels squalled against the brake blocks, and the horses' hooves plopped softly in the dust. I closed my eyes. Still we jolted downward, and I dozed, hating to miss any part of the changing scene but helpless against a stupor of drowsiness.

"We're getting down." The driver's voice woke me, and I straightened with a jerk. The road was only slightly downgrade, and the sun laced through cottonwoods. Lush grass thrust up stoutly between the rocks, and goldenrod nodded dustily. We were traveling along the floor of a narrow canyon. Widely spaced frame and log houses appeared.

"This is White Bird Creek," he said. "Runs into the Salmon near here. You won't see the river until you cross the ferry."

"I've crossed the Snake on a ferry," I said proudly. "And once I was out on it a little way in a rowboat."

"You won't do no pleasure boating on this river, ma'am. It don't take kindly to bridges or boats. Harry Guleke's the only man ever to run the Salmon in a boat. He builds a scow at Salmon City every year and runs her down to Lewiston during low water. Just sells her for lumber there. No man could ever make it up the river through them rapids. 'River of No Return' some folks calls it, poetic-like."

"I can hardly wait to see it," I said. "Folks in my part of the state seem to have heard a lot, but I couldn't find anyone who'd ever been here. They told me the horses were shod with hobnails—the mountains were that steep. And that there were wild men—fellows who'd got lost in the canyons years ago and never could find their way out. So, they just went wild."

My companion chuckled indulgently. "Most folks just talk without knowing. But it's mighty big. A man could spend his whole life trying to fit the pieces all together and still not get a good start. The river cracks the state clean from Oregon to Montana, and it's plenty wide and plenty rough and plenty deep. Look, here's yer first river town. And like I told you, there's Sanson's rig and young Brick Sanson standing there on the hotel porch all slicked up and rarin' to meet the new schoolma'am."

2

The Sanson Ranch

My trunk was unpacked. Clothes hung from nails behind the door, and my books and writing materials were arranged on the rough lumber table beside the bed. There was one prim, straight back chair with a square of cowhide tacked across the seat, a tiny sheet iron heater and a woodbox stacked with wood chunks and kindling.

I pulled the chair up to the table and began a letter to my mother. She hadn't wanted me to come—had said, "Oh, my poor child," over and over in sorrowful resignation. She must be assured that I had escaped stage robbers and scalp snatchers and was safely anchored in a little cabin only a few feet from the Sanson door. If I hurried, I could run up to the road and put the letter in the canvas bag that hung from a pole over the mailbox. A rider going into town would pick it up, and it would go out on the afternoon stage.

A shadow fell across the hewn log that was my doorstep. Mrs. Sanson stood there regarding me somberly. "I brought you an extra quilt. The nights are getting cold. And here are some pictures to brighten your walls. We should have papered this place before you came."

"Think it's nice," I said. "Everything is just fine."

She did not answer, but her eyes rested on me speculatively, almost morosely, it seemed. I had wondered ceaselessly about Mrs. Sanson that morning. She had been remote, silent, and unsmiling ever since we drove in tired and dusty the preceding evening. Perhaps it was the way she wore her hair, skinned back tightly and twisted into a hard knot at the back of her head. I wished she'd loosen it a bit. Then perhaps she could smile. She was a small person with erect bearing that gave the impression of greater stature. Her ravaged face still held traces of youthful beauty, and her eyes, deep set and smoky gray, were those of the dreamer, of one who partook of deep inner life.

"Dinner will be at two," she said. "We always plan it for that time on Sunday." Abruptly she stepped from the door and left me staring at the patch of sunlight on the floor and wondering uneasily about this strange woman with whom I was to live for the next eight months.

My letter written, I stood awhile at the mailbox and looked down on the Sanson ranch. It was the biggest piece of flat ground I had seen since we dropped down from Camas Prairie into that mass of tumbling mountains. Nor was it entirely flat, for it sloped away wedge-shaped to a point far below where the feet of two mountains seemed to meet in a tangle of trees and brush. To the right rose a rugged, bare mountain with a knob-shaped summit—Round Mountain, as I knew it later. Buck Creek flowed at its base. The left of the wedge was bounded by a small, nameless creek, and the hills rose behind it, rolling to the river.

It was a snug little ranch with its square log house surrounded by orchard and garden. It's barn, sheds, and corrals followed the downward slope. The drought of autumn was on it, but its harsh tones were softened by a haze of misty blue.

The long table in the kitchen was spread with a Sunday white cloth. Close by, on the wood range, kettles emitted appetizing odors. I hovered around trying to help. Brick came in with a bucket of water, cool from the deep well at the end of the porch. Jess Sanson, at the washstand, sloshed water, polished his ruddy face on the roller towel, and ran a comb through his reddish, graying hair.

Food was served on thick, white dishes, and we partook of the best fare I was ever to enjoy in the river country. Later I was to recall the bounty of the Sanson table with longing.

There was fried chicken; fat brown biscuits with cream gravy; mashed potatoes; corn, beans, and squash; numerous dishes of pickles, jellies, and preserves; sweet, cool melons; and deep-dish apple pie. Brick and his father talked of the cattle, the range, and probable feed conditions for the winter. Mrs. Sanson said nothing.

"Is there a short cut to the river?" I asked during a break in the conversation.

Instantly I was aware of a tenseness in the faces of the two men, and Mrs. Sanson's somber eyes stared at me fixedly.

Brick said quickly, "Sure there is. I'll show you after dinner."

"It was getting dark last night when we crossed and I didn't get to see it really," I blundered on. "I've heard such a lot about the Salmon River—"

"We'll let the beef drift in the lower pasture tonight," interrupted Jess Sanson harshly—most rudely, I thought.

Bewildered and resentful, I was silent.

Two hours later, I sat on a flat rock near the mouth of Buck Creek and looked at the river. Brick squatted on his heels and scattered gravel. Of solid and powerful build, he was an attractive study in bronze with hair like rubbed copper, a fighting chin, ruddy complexion, and that type of ice-blue eyes with the quality to spark instantly to flame-blue.

A small bar had formed where Buck Creek pushed into the mother stream, but a hundred feet across, bluffs of black rock held the river's grim course.

"It doesn't look rough," I said. "Just smooth and green like a strip of satin."

"Look close," said Brick as he threw out a twig. It danced along crazily for a second and then disappeared suddenly as if sucked down by an invisible mouth.

"No," I cried. "Now I see that it isn't quiet. It looks like water just at the boiling point. It's whirling too and moving fast."

"Plenty fast," said Brick.

Fascinated, I stared down through the clear, green depths at the huge boulders that lined its bed. There were black places, too, that looked bottomless, and here the water was furiously agitated.

"Potholes," said Brick, following my steady stare.

"I don't like it," I said at last. "It gives me the creeps—like a monster waiting to grab and pull you down."

"Look," said Brick, teetering back on his heels. "I hate to tell you this, but you'll have to know, I guess. Didn't you notice at the dinner table?"

"I only asked a simple question," I said, and started to explain when I was cut off. Are all women in this country supposed to be seen but not heard? Like—like your mother?"

"Don't get so damned uppity," said Brick, and sparks were in his eyes. "Let me explain, will you? It's just that we don't talk about the river when Mother's around. You see, my brother was drowned below here a few miles when he and my father were swimming cattle one fall."

"Oh," I faltered. "I'm sorry."

"Mother took it mighty hard. She's never been the same since. They couldn't keep her at home, and she rode up and down the river with the search party. Where she couldn't ride, she walked, and she was there when they found him and pulled him in, six days later, floating twelve miles down the river in a big eddy. The water was warm—and pounding over the rocks. You wouldn't believe that a human body could get like he was." His sturdy shoulders quivered.

I stared at the river, recalling macabre reports of similar drownings in the Snake.

"It was so bad," continued Brick, "that they had to bring him home on a travois. Mother was bound he shouldn't cross the river again to the White Bird cemetery. We had a baby sister buried here anyway, so there's two graves up by the old cabin."

"There's something comforting about being buried on your own land. I expect your mother felt that way."

"That was nine years ago. Mother sort of withdrew from everything and everybody. She's never seen the river since they found him. Won't even cross it to go to town. So that's why we quit talking about it at home."

On the path that led up to the lower pasture, I asked, "Where's the old cabin?"

"There's a trail," said Brick. "I'll show you. It's overgrown now. No one goes up there anymore. Dad built it when he homesteaded the place, and they lived there until the house was finished. Mother's always had a feeling for the old cabin. The tallest pine on the ranch grows just outside the door. Look, here's the trail, but you can't see the cabin for the trees and brush."

I made careful note of the dim trail, planning to explore further at my leisure.

3

Smoky Mule

My little one-room school was four miles up Buck Creek, and every day the Smoky mule took me there and brought me home, for after a few skirmishes, I made no attempt to rule him—just sat in the saddle and let him have his way. It was soon evident that nothing I could do, either by wheedling or firmness, had the slightest effect on him.

Jess Sanson was pitching hay into the mangers when I rode into the barn after the first day of school. He stuck the pitchfork into the hay with a deft downward thrust and scrambled over into Smoky's stall.

"How'd you make out?" he inquired. "Get all the kids lined up and toein' the mark?"

"I got along fine," I said, sliding stiffly from the saddle. "There's only six of them and all little fellows. I guess I can keep them in hand."

"Smoky behave all right?" he inquired.

"As long as he had his own way."

"Well now." he chuckled. "I told Mother that old Smoky would be your big problem at the Buck Creek School, but she was bound he'd be safer for you. And I kinda thought so too. Mules are mighty sure-footed, and that Buck Creek trail gets terrible slick at times. Of course, you can always use a saddle horse when you want to ride out."

"We took the lower trail this morning, but the children said the upper trail was so much nicer that I wanted to come home that way. I only wanted to. We came the lower trail."

"I bet," he said. "The upper trail's longer and steeper, and that Smoky mule knows it."

"He wouldn't take a step on it," I explained. "Just stood there and hung his ears. I got off and tried to lead him, and still he wouldn't move. When I turned him down the lower trail, though, he started right off."

"It takes Brick to handle him," said Jess. "He don't try no funny stuff with Brick." He slipped off the bridle and turned to unsaddle.

"Let me," I said quickly. "I ought to learn to do this for myself." I could see that pleased him. He stood back while I fumbled with the cinch.

"You make mighty hard work of it. Just pull that end and the loop falls through. That's right. Wait now. Don't leave the latigo hanging like that. It trails through the dirt and gets all messed up; loop it through the cinch ring. I'll lift it off for you and show you how to hang it up. Brick's fussy about the saddles. Don't like 'em hung by a stirrup like some folks do."

He carried the saddle over to where several ropes hung from a rafter each with a loop in its end. "Loop comes up through here. See? Then back around the saddle horn. That leaves the saddle swing free."

"It's a nice saddle," I said, "and comfortable. But even so, I bet I'll be stiff tomorrow."

His brown hands caressed the smooth leather. "Brick bought this saddle with the first money he ever made ridin'. Bought it for his ma. But," he added softly, "she's never used it more'n a dozen times."

"Where's Brick?" I asked casually.

"Went ridin' today for Wynn. They're roundin' up beef on the forest reserve and in the Doumecq country. He'll be gone a spell."

The next morning, I took a firm attitude with the Smoky mule. He was really a beautiful animal when he held up his head and ears. But he delighted to poke along, head down and huge ears flopping. When I tried to hold him up with a tight rein, he stopped and refused to move further. In vain, I slapped him hard with the reins. He only hunched himself and planted his small hooves more firmly on the trail. So, I let that pass, and we went flopping along until we neared the fork to the upper trail, where I made another stand. Twisting off a switch from an overhanging alder, I struck him sharply. He made a deceptive burst of speed and headed into the lower trail, maintaining a smart gait until it was too late to turn back. If this went on, I decided, the brute would take me anywhere whenever he pleased. That evening, there'd be a showdown. There was.

When I came to the forks on the homeward trek, I turned his head into the uptrail and switched him smartly. We stood firm as a rock. I switched harder and again harder. No effect. Then I got off, thinking to win him with guile. I picked some tender young grass and brought it to him. He blew on it disdainfully. Then I talked to him, using some hard words but in a low and persuasive voice. His eyelids drooped indifferently, and he hung his lower lip. Again, I offered the grass. This time he snatched it ungraciously, wasting most of it in the dust. I tugged on the reins toward the upper trail. He flexed himself and stood his ground. I wondered how long he would stand there and wondered if I could stick it out with him.

I sat down on a big rock that jutted out into the trail and leaned back against the bank. Buck Creek and the base of Round Mountain already lay in shadow. The hush of evening was broken only by a faint sighing in the tall pines that sentineled the upper trail. Again, I envisioned that limitless jungle of mountains I had seen from the edge of the prairie. Those that hemmed me in now were only one tiny sector of the enormous whole. I must remember that awesome panorama-must see it always as a whole, not just a tiny pocket where I had found a temporary stopping place. What of this vast, rugged gorge? Its people? The sinister but fascinating river that formed its nucleus? The old stage driver's words came back to me: "Splits the State. Plenty wide and plenty rough and plenty deep. This don't hold a candle to the upper river, but I don't reckon you'll ever see it. Spend a whole life and never get the pieces all together."

I must have sat there a long time, gripped in the solitude of this wild and mysterious hinterland. Shadows had crept far up on the Round Mountain when I remembered my present problem. Suddenly my feud with Smoky seemed silly and pointless—sitting doggedly, trying to outstubborn a balky mule. The poor fellow must be hungry standing all day tied in the little shed back of the schoolhouse with nothing in his stomach but a drink of water at noon. I jumped up, threw the reins over his obstinate head, and clambered into the saddle.

"The best man wins, fellow," I said. "That's you."

He wheeled quickly and stepped down on the lower trail at a brisk pace. He was headed for oats and hay.

We never argued over the trail again. Always after that when we came to the forks, he'd quicken his pace, pick up his ears, and let one dip insinuatingly toward the upper trail. Words couldn't have said more plainly, "There it is. What are you going to do about it?"

4

Pocket of Peace

Half of the rambling log barn was crammed with hay, and there was a hollow just above the mangers where one could burrow down into a snug nest. Through the wide door, brown slopes fell away toward the Salmon. Here and there, bushes flared with October brilliance. A thin haze softened the sharp ridges, and over it all hung an aura of peace and contentment. Mike, the shepherd dog, appeared in the door, sniffed inquiringly, and waved his plume briskly at sight of me. He approached ingratiatingly, his whole body awag. Then with the low manger between us, he paused and studied me questioningly.

"Come on, Mike," I said. "Come on up."

Joyously he leaped the manger and nestled down beside me. His nose sought my lunch sack, and he inhaled with long sniffs. I opened it and fed him the remnants of sandwiches and a few cake crumbs. He was this country's typical stock dog—a border collie, small but agile, black coated and stockinged in tan with tan dots above his eyes and a handsome throat latch of the same hue. I stroked his soft coat and worked at a matted burr.

The gray barn cat appeared suddenly on a feed box and studied us uncertainly. Her tail arose straight and crooked a little at the end as she balanced herself daintily. She jumped down and cautiously approached. I stretched out my hand to coax her into our intimate circle, but Mike rose jealously and nudged her away. She leaped over the manger and stalked to the door, turned her back to us, and sat down to observe a group of scratching hens. Mike sighed deeply, turned to me with an air of satisfaction, and relaxed against my shoulder.

Smoky and the work team crunched their feed, and we all drowsed there in peace with only the switching of tails and the plump of a hoof against the barn floor to break our lazy dreaming. What a little world within itself, this remote ranch—truly a kingdom, with its crops, its animals, its trees and streams.

The jingle of bridle chains and the ring of a shod hoof against stone brought me up from my fragrant nest. I brushed the hay from my riding skirt, snatched up my lunch sack, and walked sedately to the door. I thought it might be Brick, home from roundup, but it wasn't. It was Jess Sanson riding Taffy, his buckskin mare, and with him was a stranger, looking out of place in city clothes and a narrow-brimmed felt hat. They rode straight past the barn to the water trough where they sat relaxed while the horses drank. Talking earnestly, they didn't notice me, and I walked with Mike slowly up to the house.

Fruit trees arched the path, and the ground was studded with apples in bright reds and yellows. I stooped to select one, and Mike watched me bite into it with begging eyes. I offered him a bit, and he turned away in offended dignity. Then the wondrous odor of freshly baked bread wafted down from the house. I dropped the half-eaten apple and directed my steps toward the kitchen.

A place was laid at the supper table for the stranger. He was the Utah Woolen Mills salesman whose territory was the Salmon and who made his visit once a year to homes along the lower river country. No peddler he, but an honored guest whose contacts with the outside world set him apart. His opinions were received with respectful attention. Exponent of progress, his ideas were a confused reflection of that day so perilously close to the nation's plunge into war. This man, President Wilson, he said, had vowed to keep us out of it, but our ships were sinking. Let us keep our cargoes home, he urged. America for Americans.

After supper, his wares, samples, and pictured folders were spread out for inspection. Selections were a matter of grave concern. Jess Sanson fingered the soft wools. They clung to his work-hard fingers. He passed them to Mrs. Sanson, who observed them silently. Jess would have black woolen union suits and a heavy stag shirt. Mrs. Sanson chose a blanket and a blue flannel shirt for Brick. The order was written and the tempo of conversation settled down to man talk. It shuttled between the faraway world of mills and men at machines to the inside world between the canyon walls.

5

Pay Day

Smoky swelled himself mightily to obstruct cinching, and I waited with scant patience for the opportunity to give another quick tug on the strap. His performance was unusually irritating that day, for it was Saturday, marking the end of my first school month, and I was impatient to be on my way to White Bird. The trip was to be quite an event, for I had gone nowhere and seen few people except Jess and Lydia Sanson and my six pupils. Activity at that season centered on the high ranges, and it had been a quiet month on the river. I felt gay and adventurous, for in my pocket was a salary warrant for fifty dollars, the first money I had ever earned and a princely sum, it seemed to me.

Smoky's gray coat was sleek from brush and curry comb, his roach freshly trimmed. I decided to use Brick's best bridle. It was a handsome affair with silver conchas on the headstall and braided rawhide reins, which were joined to form a long, graceful Romal, useful as an instrument of persuasion.

We'd cantered smartly up the drive that led to the road when I saw Mrs. Sanson standing at the gate. I pulled up and sat there silently while her steady eyes studied me and the Smoky mule.

"You're sure you know the way?" she asked.

"Of course. I still remember from the day I came. You just follow along until you come to the ferry. I couldn't get lost."

"Be careful," she said.

"I will," and I added gently. "Is there something I can bring you from town?"

"Nothing," she said simply and turned away.

Smoky and I followed the twisting road down. Down between the brown hills, across dry creek beds, around stern outcrops of lava, and over brief flats covered with parched grass. Insects chorused from weedy thickets, and faintly, somewhere back in the high hills, came the distant lowing of cattle. Down, down through the sere slopes to the river and a long sand flat where floodwater had deposited nests of drift in willow clumps.

The ferry was hardly more than a shaky platform on pontoons with a flimsy rail of poles and a hinged apron at each end to ensure an incline to the bank. The ferryman, a grizzled old fellow with flowing mustache, had seen us coming far up the road, for he was waiting for us, ready to cast off when we rode aboard. The ferry was attached by ropes and pulleys to a guy-wire stretched across the river, and it took strenuous pulling on the ropes to get us out in the current. Once there, we scuttled swiftly across.

"I'll be back after a while," I said. "We'll make it a round trip. I'll pay you then."

My pilot lowered the apron, smiled, and nodded. We clattered gaily off and up the dusty road to the town. Smoky must have sensed my elation, for he threw up his head, set his ears alertly, and stepped out with a beautiful, swinging walk. His tiny hooves seemed scarcely to touch the earth. Conscious of his smart appearance, I sat my saddle with erect dignity as we swung up the one and only street.

Saturdays always brought the mountain people and the river folk alike to White Bird. They came on horseback or in family groups in buckboards or surreys. The hitching racks were lined with teams and saddle horses. I saw no mule under saddle, but I didn't wonder about it then. How was I to know that mules were not considered fashionable mounts, were used mainly in the high trail country, rarely ridden by women, and certainly never to town? I noticed that we were being curiously stared at. People along the street gazed back at us after we had passed. The crowd of men lounging on the porch of the general store stopped talking and gave careful attention to our progress. I was sure they were admiring Smoky, who by now was prancing along with dainty, mincing steps. Between the bank and the hotel where the loungers were the thickest, Smoky came to a sudden dead halt.

"What now?" I murmured, "Smoky, you fool, go on." And I nudged him sharply in the ribs.

Instead, he appeared to swell, and there was a curious vibration through his body. It felt as if he were on the point of exploding under me. He's sick, I thought desperately. I had visions of him falling dead with me in the street. Appealingly, I sought the groups of widely grinning faces. The vibrations reached a crescendo, and the Smoky mule burst into song. His hee-haws blasted the quiet of the river town.

Grins gave way to hearty laughter. Everyone but me, it appeared, was being hugely entertained. In shame and disgust, I dug heels fiercely into Smoky's ribs and slapped him with the romal. But he wasn't through, and not a step would he move until the business was finished. At last the bray died down weakly and faded to a simpering squeak. He shook himself gently and ambled on, all his fire and elation gone.

Flushed and humiliated, I hung my head, and we moved meekly up the street, on past the business section, anywhere out of the sight of those laughing people. Where the houses that fronted the thoroughfare were widely spaced, I rode aside and dismounted by a clump of chokecherry bushes. I regarded the Smoky mule more in sadness than with anger, and he too hung his head, his ears in a dejected droop. I left him drowsing there, tied to the bushes. Slowly I walked back into town and cashed my check at the bank. No one seemed to notice me. Without Smoky, I was inglorious.

My enthusiasm for exploring the town had departed. I imagined myself to be the object of secret, pitying looks. Even the anticipated joy of the roll of bills tucked in my pocket had faded. I looked about the little town with its boardwalks, its false fronted stores, and its groups of roughly clad people and thought how ugly everything was. For me, had departed, all the glamour of that bright October day.

I wandered back to Smoky, but here a new problem

presented itself. Going back down the street, he might repeat the performance, and I felt unable to endure a curtain call. Bleakly, I considered a possible escape by devious paths to avoid the main street. What looked like a possible trail led off across White Bird Creek close up under the rocky walls of its canyon. But Smoky would have none of that. We had taken less than a dozen steps along the path when he planted himself and refused to budge.

"Smoky," I cried. "I could beat your ears off and love it."

There was nothing to do but to make a main street exit.

"All right, fella," I said. "If we have to, we're going right through."

I swung the rawhide romal in a vicious arc around Smoky's rear. Snorting indignantly, he leaped forward with a suddenness that nearly unseated me, but holding the saddle horn firmly, I righted myself and delivered another stinging lick. Under the urge of such persuasion, we galloped madly through town and disappeared in a cloud of dust.

Afterward I was told that my departure was fully as entertaining as my entrance, and I have no doubt such was the case, for when we at last stopped at the ferry my shirt tail had pulled out and fluttered behind me, my riding skirt had worked itself up to a sightly line above my knees, and my hat was left behind somewhere in the dust of the road.

6

Wilderness Water

The Salmon drops a vertical mile from its glacial source to its junction with the Snake. It is Idaho's own water, every one of its tributaries having their source within the state. Its four hundred-mile course swings free of any city, and a consistent work pattern marks its sweep. From its origin in the lofty Sawtooth peaks and past the Pahsimeroi on to the evil stretches of Snow Hole Rapids and the rugged walls of Blue Canyon at its union with the Snake, it follows the work line of stock raising and mining.

In its upper course, it brawls through rugged wilderness, gathering reinforcements for its cut into the continent's greatest granite mass. In this frenzied attack, it has hewn a six thousand feet gorge from rim to river. It is deadly with rapids, and the few quiet stretches are foam-flecked with its madness.

At its juncture with the Little Salmon, it takes an abrupt north turn. Here is the town of Riggins. From here, on past White Bird, the canyon widens, and the water becomes more docile. Mountain flanks replace granite bluffs, and alluvial bars are frequent. River ranches dot this stretch, where small blocks of alfalfa promise winter feed for cattle, which range up the mountains to the high meadows for summer grazing.

The brief peace of the river breaks as it approaches its confluence with the Snake. The canyon pinches in and becomes vertical and forbidding. The river resumes its willful savagery, and foaming stretches of white water batter against rocks, which rear up in midstream. The chasm's basic granite formation gives way to lava, rising step like in dizzy heights to dark and somber pinnacles. When the river enters Blue Canyon, it has received all its main tributaries. Its arrogance increases as it tears through this last gorge to its rendezvous with the Snake.

7

Thaddeus of Horn Creek

Where the road left the hills, and wound over the sandy bar to the ferry, a small creek had hewn a diminutive gorge to the Salmon. Wearied by its long plunge, its high-water burdens were laid down to form a small bar studded with boulders. A steep path led down from the road to a boxlike shack of rough lumber. Strips of buckskin were nailed over the vertical cracks between the boards. The wood, darkened by weather and the buckskin whitened by the same agent, gave it a striped appearance. Under the extended shake roof sheltering its door was nailed a bleaching spread of deer horns. Where the path forked from the road, a magnificent pine grew and on it was fastened a neat mailbox; above it, a carefully carved sign, Horn Creek; below in faint penciling, Thaddeus G. Horn.

It was a dreary Saturday in late November when I noted for the first time, smoke coming from the shack's rusty stovepipe. I was riding to White Bird aboard Smokey, my first return venture since the braying incident. The lingering Indian summer had been suddenly snuffed out, and for two days it had rained steadily. The clouds hung low, the trees dripped, and the road was heavy. I was riding with what grudging speed

Smoky would make, anxious to arrive before the upriver mail left for Riggins. At the Horn mailbox stood a man, and he was certainly flagging me down. I pulled up in a spindrift of mud.

An old gentleman neatly clad in plaid mackinaw, corduroys, and high-laced boots was holding up a canvas bag. "Are you coming back this way, stranger?" he asked. Crinkles formed at the corners of his merry blue eyes. Raindrops clung to his mustache, and there was a fringe of white hair under his corduroy cap.

"Why, yes," I said. "Shall I bring your mail?"

"Excuse me, ma'am," he said, removing his cap. "I didn't realize I was addressing a lady."

"Think nothing of it." I laughed. "My own mother wouldn't claim me in this outfit!" I was clad in Jess Sanson's oilskin poncho—a big square, centered with a hole to thrust one's head through; it hung to my stirrups. My costume was further enhanced by a beaver cap styled on Cossack lines. Moth-eaten but warm and waterproof, it was a relic of Jess's youthful fur-trading excursions. I had pushed my hair up into its simple crown, and it was no wonder that the old man had mistaken me for a scarecrow youth. I reached down for the bag, fretting at the delay.

"I'll be back this afternoon with your mail, Mr. Horn."

"Just the letters, if you will." He held the cap to his breast and bowed slightly.

As the road curved to the river bar, I glanced back. Thaddeus Horn still stood there bareheaded in the rain, staring after us.

If White Bird felt playful, a good laugh was due this day, I decided. I was well spattered with mud, and Smoky's belly and running gear were caked and dripping. Thus plastered, he looked skinny, rat-tailed, and all ears. But the town appeared not in a festive mood. It was dreary, drenched, and deserted. Brazenly I nudged Smoky between the scattering of saddle horses at the post office hitching rack. I stepped down into a sea of mud and up on the scant strip of boardwalk.

When I presented the Horn mail sack, the spritely oldster in charge of federal affairs began reaching for bundles of newspapers tied with twine.

"Thad's back, eh?" His bright bird-like eyes peered through the bars of the little window. "Did he find that gold mine?"

"He didn't say, and I didn't know he was looking for one."

"Never leaves off lookin' till the snow drives him back to the river," he stated, thrusting bundles into the sack.

"He's got a heap of mail," I ventured, eyeing the sizable sack now filled to the draw rope.

"Just about half of it," he trilled cheerfully, picking up an empty sack from the corner and again reaching for the bundles.

"Look here," I announced stoutly, "I haven't a packhorse. I can't carry so much on my saddle."

"Thad'll be mighty disappointed if he don't get it. It's been piling up here for six months." He drew the rope on the second sack, dragged both out the door, and deposited them at my feet. Briskly, he dusted his hands and regarded me alertly like an aggressive cock sparrow.

"I can't carry all that," I repeated doggedly.

"They weigh light," he chirped. "Nothin' but newspapers and such. Thad's a great reader. I'll haul 'em out for you. Hang one on each side from the saddle horn."

He hopped out the door dragging the sacks, and I followed, protesting that Thad only wanted the letters.

"Letters!" he piped. "There ain't no letters. He's always imaginin' he's goin' to have letters."

It was evident that the "sparrow man" was determined to rid himself of the mass of mail and me at one fell swoop. The bags were indeed already slung on the saddle, and he had buzzed back into the office. Resignedly I climbed aboard, impeded by the bags, which bulged hugely on each side like overstuffed panniers.

I gathered the poncho over myself and the freight; jammed the beaver headgear far down over my ears; and faced the bitter, wind-driven rain that swept down the river. No more trips to White Bird without a bodyguard, I decided. This was the end.

Smoky, homeward bound, was for getting there and fast. My cargo flopped, and I flopped; the wind pried under the poncho, and it flopped and soared out behind like a horizontal sail. I used secret profanity in reference to the "sparrow man" for hanging this wretched load on us and also to Mr. Thaddeus Horn and his voracious appetite for reading.

As we rode down the trail to the door of the Horn cabin, Thad stepped out, and a teasing odor of brewing coffee followed him. He looked horrified when he saw my load.

"Young lady," he said sorrowfully, "I had no intention that you should have been burdened in this fashion. I hoped only for my letter mail."

His courtly manner and the real distress in his voice prompted me to lie glibly. It was no bother at all, I assured him, and the mail was all bundled together so the letters weren't segregated. I couldn't bear to tell the old fellow that he had no letters. He lifted the sacks down under the shelter of the overhanging roof.

"You will step down and have a cup of coffee," he stated.

I decided that I would. He threw a strip of canvas over my saddle, drew Smoky under the roof, and hung my dripping poncho outside the door.

"An ugly day for a young lady to be riding," he said bowing me into his domicile. "You have come here since I left last spring, surely."

"I'm teaching at Buck Creek," I said and gave him my name.

"Interesting," he said. "Kay Wong. It has an oriental sound."

"No, I said quickly, "not Wong, Wonn." And I spelled it.

"Ah, yes, quite so." He nodded and smiled.

Hard of hearing, I decided, and trying bravely to hide the fact; but the intent way he watched my lips and the turn of his head betrayed it.

"Did you find the gold mine?" I inquired politely, seating myself on a bench flanking a rough board table and accepting gratefully a steaming cup of black coffee.

"I have the most excellent prospects," he exclaimed jubilantly. "I was on the verge of a great strike when the weather became too threatening for further work. Let me show you."

From a jumble of packing equipment, he dragged forth a canvas sack and began piling ore specimens on the table. He pulled a magnifying glass from his pocket and began reading the story of locked wealth in terms utterly meaningless to me.

"Now this," he exclaimed with sparkling eyes, "is certainly from the great vein that I was just on the verge of locating. It will assay one thousand to the ton. A fitting reward for these many years of search!"

"You must have been here a long time," I said loudly, "to have a creek named for you."

"I hear perfectly, Miss Wong," he said. "You need not raise your voice. Yes, eighteen years ago, I came here, fancied this small bar, and camped. The creek, Miss Wong, was not named for me. Dear no! But on this cabin site, I found a fine set of deer horns. And since the stream was nameless, I decided it should be known as Horn Creek, in honor of that fine spread of horns. You may have noticed it over my door."

He regarded me hopefully, waiting for my response. I nodded and smiled. Looking pleased, he turned again to the disordered pack equipment and began searching earnestly.

The dour day was deepening into twilight. The rain drove against the cabin's single window and beat busily on the unsealed roof. A rusty camp stove was the only accent of cheer in the room. Embers glowed through seams in the firebox, and occasionally rain dripped down by the stovepipe to sizzle and dance on its surface. On a bunk against the wall, a bedroll had been spread. One corner of the room was stacked with dusty newspapers, books, and magazines. It all seemed incredibly lonely, cheerless, and depressing.

Thad retuned to the table with a small bottle, nearly full of a yellowish, grainy substance and spread its contents on a sheet of paper. Gold dust and nuggets. There were several of the latter, the largest about the size of a grain of corn.

"My panning's," he announced carelessly. "One has to look to the immediate necessities."

"How lovely," I said, touching them carefully with a forefinger. "Here's one all crinkled and with a piece of gravel caught in the folds."

"Please select one for your own," he said.

"No, I couldn't," I said quickly. This pitiful pile was perhaps the old man's grub stake for an entire year.

"I insist," he said with a disparaging gesture toward the exhibit. "That's nothing, Miss Wong—a miserable pittance. But next year I will indeed have something to show you. Please do me the honor."

It was a command, and beneath it lay a deep, fierce pride. Unhappily, I chose the tiny nugget with the gravel in its claw. He wrapped it in a bit of paper, and I pinned it in my shirt pocket.

"I shall keep it always," I said.

He beamed with pride. "Someday, you shall tell your friends, "This was given to me by Thaddeus G. Horn just before he made the great strike."

I could hear Smoky moving from side to side and pawing impatiently.

"I must go," I said rising. "It's getting dark, and Mrs. Sanson will worry."

"I hope you will stop again," he said. "Then we may discuss the affairs of the world and the condition of man. It is not good, I fear." He shook his head sadly. "Rumors of war. For half the year I hear little of these matters. In the winter, I catch up with the times."

Promising that I would indeed stop again, I donned the poncho; mounted Smoky, who nearly leaped from under me in his fret to be going; and took to the dreary grade of mud that lay ahead to the ranch.

In later years when I roamed the gold country, I used to inquire of Thad. No one knew him, and no one had heard of any great strike. I came to know many of his brethren, for they are legion in the high country of the Salmon. Few were as clean, as courtly, or as articulate as Thad; all were proud, fiercely independent, and spoke not of whence they came nor from what people they had cast themselves adrift. The prospectors and placer miners usually came to the river settlements or to the old mining camps for the winter. But most of the hard-rock boys sat it out on their claims, snow locked in the high mountains interlacing the smaller canyons that lunge to the river. On what lofty gold trail Thad had set his course, I shall never know. One old prospector is an infinitesimal speck in that vast labyrinth of mountains; chasms; plunging torrents; and high, lonely meadows that break the state jaggedly from the Snake to the Bitterroot range that extends along the Idaho-Montana border.

8

A Bachelor Entertains

It was two days before Christmas and my birthday. I was seventeen, a matter that gave me no comfort being still a year short of my greatly desired goal.

A light snow dusted the lower river country. The mountains were white, and a low ceiling of gray clouds hid their upper reaches. With sure, quick steps Smoky picked his way over the frozen trail. We were homeward bound, and a one-week vacation began the next day, but the prospect brought no elation. My eyes swept the lonely, gray vastness, and a lump rose in my throat. For weeks, I had figured hopefully. But it all added up to the same result—three days to Boise, three days to return. It was a no-go, and I was stuck on the Salmon River for the holidays. Engulfed in my first real attack of homesickness, I thought of the bright lights and parties. A tear trickled down my cheek and fell on my heavy wool glove.

Brick had been home since Thanksgiving. He was at the barn when I rode in and slipped from the saddle, stiff with cold.

"Want to go dancing?" he inquired.

I considered this with slight enthusiasm. Brick had taken me to the Thanksgiving Dance at White Bird. A lanky cowboy had no sooner swung me out on the floor than he's inquired if I wasn't the "schoolma'am who rode the mule." Others inquired solicitously of my mount's health and his fine tenor voice. I answered with quips and laughter as Brick had advised, but inwardly I was raging.

"If it's at White Bird, I don't want to go," I said. Brick knew full well why.

"You don't have to ride Smoky," he said. "I've told you a dozen times. You can have your pick of any well-broke horse on the place."

"I will ride him though," I said resolutely. "I'll ride him everywhere I go. I'll show them!"

"Oh, hell!" muttered Brick in disgust.

"Where's the dance?" I asked with pretended indifference.

"Pittsburg Landing. And it isn't just a dance. It's a house party, I guess you'd say. Old bachelor Mike Thomas has open house during the holidays. Everyone's welcome. Folks who are going to stay through usually take a packhorse with grub, but we'd come back tomorrow."

"All right, I'll go," I said. "And I'll ride Smoky."

"Yeah," he said. "I guess you will; you'll be traveling real mule country."

We left the ranch at noon the next day. I was bundled to the teeth—overshoes, mackinaw, riding skirts stuffed into Jess Sanson's batwing leather chaps. Behind me on the saddle was a bundle wrapped in a strip of oilcloth. Besides necessities, it contained my best dress, mauve silk with chiffon sleeves, and my precious dancing slippers. I cringed when Brick tied it on and the leather thongs bit the soft bundle.

Brick rode his Danny, mate to Smoky but so nervous and jumpy that I was never allowed on him. We traveled the wagon road to its end at the Wynn ranch and then climbed steadily single file on a narrow trail that led ever up. Soon we were in the forest reserve. Fine dry snow sifted down, covering Smoky's stiff roach with a ridge of white. Brick, in the lead, called back to me at intervals. Otherwise, the silence was unbroken except for the clink of bridle chains and the occasional ring of shod hooves on the stony trail. The wind died down in the heavy timber, but the snow still fell, mantling a world of giant Christmas trees. The gray afternoon deepened into Christmas Eve.

On the summit, a sharp wind began to blow. Behind us, the watershed sloped down to the Salmon in a sea of gray obscurity. Ahead, somewhere, we would plunge downward over rim rock through the canyon of the Snake. Some twenty miles along that divide was the final wedge where the two rivers unite.

The descent to the Snake was slow. Loose shale with its light cover of snow was deceptive but Smoky's sure feet never stumbled. It was bitterly cold. Relief came when Brick signaled me to follow and turned up a side trail to a small cabin, the first sight of human habitation since we had left the Wynn ranch. It was a forest ranger's cabin, deserted now for the winter.

"Want to call the ferry at Pittsburg Landing so's they'll be expecting us. Hate to be stuck this side of the Snake."

"Do we have to cross the river to get to the Thomas place?" I inquired forlornly. Dismounting, I stamped up and down the lean-to porch to start circulation in my numbed feet.

Brick cranked busily at the telephone. It was a party line, and many greetings were exchanged before we got Mike's place.

The trail from the ranger station became steeper. We traveled a narrow shelf hewn from sheer rock wall. The deepening twilight added to my apprehension. If Smoky should stumble! Feeling panic, I forced myself to stop watching the trail and fixed my attention on the dim outline of Brick and Danny. A bitter wind swept up the canyon.

The ferry was on the Idaho side. It looked a twin to the one at White Bird. Across the river on a bluff, a group of low buildings huddled. Lamplight streamed from the windows onto the light skiff of snow. We reined in the mules, and Brick shouted greetings to a couple of figures on the ferry.

"We've been waiting for you," one shouted. "Ice has been coming down all day. Getting bad."

"Can we make it?" called Brick.

"We can try. Other side's a tougher landing."

The Snake ran wide and black. As we rode on the ferry, the lantern light gleamed on swiftly moving ice chunks. I dismounted and stood by the pole rail, watching the widening water toward the Idaho side. We seemed a long-time crossing. As we neared the Oregon shore, Brick shouted, "Ice is backed up around that eddy. We'll have to push through with poles."

The ferry had stalled now by the slush and ice flow, which, milled in an eddy and backed up across the path of the ferry. Brick and one of the ferrymen seized long poles and began to push the ice blocks aside while the other man pulled on the rope that ran through the pulley on the guy-wire. We made no progress.

"We'll swim it," said Brick. "That will lighten her, and you can pull in."

I was up on Smoky by that time, feeling a little sick by the prospect ahead. It was twenty feet at least to the landing, and I knew beneath the slush and ice, the black water ran deep. Smoky knew what was coming. He threw his ears forward and planted his hooves firmly on the plank floor. Brick, on Danny, was crowding us to the edge of the ferry apron.

"Hold on!" shouted Brick.

I heard his romal sing through the air, landing with a vicious crack on Smoky's rear. In we went, the first plunge carrying the water to my hips. I never was a screamer, but as in a dreadful dream, I heard my own hoarse shouting mingled with Smoky's sharp snorts and Danny threshing through the water beside me. Smoky struck out for the shore. I felt him come out of swimming water to the rocky river bottom. Up on the bank, icy and dripping, Brick rode in close.

"Are you, all right?" he inquired anxiously.

"No, I'm not," I snapped waspishly. "I'm frozen, and a chunk of ice hit me on the knee. I'm tired and hungry, and I wish to heaven I'd never come. Swell way to spend Christmas Eve! Swimming Snake River in the dark and cold!"

"You're soft!" commented Brick scornfully.

My furious retort was unheard for Brick cut in with a, "Halloo".

"Here comes Mike down the hill with a lantern," he explained. "Nice guy, Mike."

Later when I was dried, warm and well fed with roast venison, potatoes, and sourdough biscuits, I had to admit it wasn't so bad after all. Mike was a dear, and no mistake, you could see he was pleased to have a house full of folks enjoying themselves. He sat enthroned in a chair close to the musicians, and his sharp eyes didn't miss anything that went on. The simple friendliness of my host and his guests made the weary trip worthwhile. I felt I had known them for years. The orchestra consisted of fiddle, accordion, and harmonica, and the musicians were tireless. Square dances, waltzes, and Paul Jones—round and round we went. There were seven women and more than twice as many men, so there were no wallflowers. We stopped to eat again at midnight, and the dance went on.

When dawn began to gray the windows, the forest ranger's

wife led me up a ladder to a loft above the big room. Bedding had been spread on the floor, and several youngsters were there asleep. This was sanctuary for the women and children. The men took themselves to the bunkhouse. My bundled dancing attire had never been unwrapped. It felt soggy from the plunge into the Snake. I slipped it under the blankets to serve as a pillow and crept into the melee of coarse bedding, fully clothed except for my shoes.

The dawn of Christmas morning pushed through the grimy attic windows. Utter exhaustion closed my eyes and mind to all traditions, to all the memories of Christmas mornings I had known.

9

"Slick Weather"

The Sanson kitchen was long and low beamed. The shaded kerosene lamp made a pool of brightness on the table's white, oilcloth cover. Winter evening activity centered on that table. Jess Sanson sat close to the range, where he could occasionally shove sticks of wood into the fiery bed of coals. Brick braided a rawhide lariat. It was a long and tedious task. Frequently, he showed me rope tricks, how to fashion a hackamore from a length of hemp and the various knots useful in working with horses and cattle.

I read, wrote letters, or looked at the mail order catalogues. Brick sometimes joined me over the pages of those from the saddleries. We examined each illustration carefully, read the descriptions over and over, and compared prices. I respected his authoritative opinions on riding equipment. Jess Sanson did not and was apt to point out the superior trappings of an earlier day. Or he launched into tales of cattle and trails and the men who fought those trails, their animals, and each other. Sometimes he sang "The Dying Cowboy" and a long, woeful saga of the Chisholm Trail.

Mrs. Sanson combed wool for comforters or darned and mended. She took no interest in any of the catalogues, other than ordering from them once each year the household and personal necessities. Occasionally she glanced over the *Idaho County Free Press*, but her reading seemed mainly confined to two books, the Bible and Thoreau's <u>Walden.</u> I considered both extremely dull. She read slowly and thoughtfully between long periods of meditation, utterly withdrawn from us. Physically, our daily lives gravitated to her; spiritually, she walked alone in a world naked of the values by which we lived. At the time, I thought of her pityingly as a lonely, unhappy woman. Now I know that she was not and never would be.

In late winter came bad days for the cattlemen. It was so every year in the canyon country, and many cattle were lost if allowed on steep range at that time. It was a condition laconically described as "slick weather." Jess Sanson was worried and kept asking Brick if he were sure all their cattle were in, off Round Mountain.

"Sure are," said Brick. "But there's Wynn beef in there yet, and they'll roll, sure, if it keeps on many days like this."

"Let 'em," grunted his father. "Any outfit that careless! A dozen riders layin' up there in the bunkhouse. Old Wynn out in Spokane bright-lighting around and their critters scattered all over the range."

Jess didn't approve of the Wynn outfit. He was the small fry rancher, and Wynn represented big interests and special privilege. Never did he let an opportunity pass to challenge and criticize his big-time neighbor.

Brick told me how cattle "rolled" on the steep mountains when the ground was frozen. During sunny days, it softened a little on top but remained hard beneath. The hungry cattle searching for tufts of dry bunch grass often lost their footing and went crashing down the bare, steep mountain in a horrible manner—something I was to witness before "slick weather" gave way to a general thaw.

It was on an afternoon in early February, and Smoky was taking me home. He picked his way carefully, for the sun shone warmly, and it was surely slick on the trail. Cattle had rolled that week, for a couple of Wynn riders were in the bottoms at the base of Round Mountain skinning the carcasses that were fit to dehide. There were two cows far up on the mountain, and I watched them anxiously.

I was too far away to recognize the beginning of the fatal slip. I saw only that the creature farthest up began to slide, and I heard it bawl in frantic terror as it braced its forelegs and sat on its rump in a vain effort to break speed and regain footing. Almost never do they do so. As it gained momentum, it began to bounce; the bounces became prodigious leaps as the mass of flesh and crushed bone neared the base of the mountain. The last sickening projection into space hid it from my view in the clumps of willows bordering Buck Creek.

The only visible sign of the swift tragedy was a dark line measuring the upper length of the death slide. There must have been many pitiful bodies in that creek bottom. A feeling of revulsion for this stark, ruthless country swept over me.

When spring thaws rushed the snow waters to the Salmon, all evidence would be swept away, and I envisioned the great river in high water with its cargo of death contributed to by its countless feeder streams such as Buck Creek.

10

Rider from the Seven Devils

The Sanson place was a landmark, and Jess Sanson was himself a maker of historical events on the Salmon River. He had fought in the Nez Perce Indian war of 1877, then a mere youngster who had won his spurs on the cattle drives of the Chisholm Trail and whose restlessness urged him west to the music of the then unknown Salmon River country. The sturdy log house was built in the late 1880s and, for many years, was a stopping place on the trail between the forks of the Salmon and the Snake. Still hardly a week passed that some rider was not there for meals and a night's lodging.

One raw March night, a man rode in from the Norton ranch in the Seven Devils' country and adventure rode with him. He was the pictured westerner in person, tall in his high-heeled boots and wearing his rough garb with unpretending grace. He sat up to the warmed-over supper, and we all gathered around the table. He and Brick and Jess Sanson had many mutual friends. They talked of the trails—of cattle and feed conditions, of people who lived along those trails, and of their fortunes and misfortunes with their cattle.

As I sat gazing across the lamp-lit table at this talkative young stranger, a new sector of this great country came into focus. It was Hells Canyon of the Snake, and except for the few who peopled its forbidding stretches, almost none knew it. Mindful of my absorbed attention, young Norton launched with fervor into his subject—sturgeon fishing on the Snake. "Caught one last year bigger than a yearling calf." The canyon? "Yes, it was really a hole in the rock, seven thousand nine hundred feet from He-Devil Peak to the river."

"Deeper than the Colorado," I exclaimed in awe.

"Reckon so," he said. "You being a schoolteacher ought to know. A survey party gave these figures on Hells Canyon last summer."

He talked on, and I listened intently.

"There's a school," he said, "at the breaks of the canyon—on the Oregon side. Summer school, too. Four months, I think. Hear they're looking for a teacher."

"Who," I questioned earnestly, "are the school directors, and what is the address?"

Out in my cabin, I started a fire and sat down to write my letter. Doubts slowed my progress. My mother would be deeply disappointed if I failed to come home at the end of my present term. It would be well to improve my teaching technique with a summer course. My friends would believe me addled to deliberately spend additional time in this uncharted wilderness. Definitely, after a term in a country school, one was supposed to have acquired enough experience to be rewarded with a city position or at least a place on the fringe of civilization. But for me, such alternatives had no allure. I decided to take another flyer into the unknown.

No other in my profession seemed to have any such wild urge. The speed with which my application was accepted surprised me, and I was entranced by the salary, exceeding the Buck Creek figure by twenty dollars a month.

"Sure fell for that Norton guy, didn't you?" Brick remarked hatefully when I announced my election.

"I could have," I retorted, "but I'll probably never see him again."

As it turned out, I never did, but its possibility continued to be a subject for frequent needling by Brick. Our bickering was interspersed with brief interludes of romancing, but always these tender episodes erupted into conflict. Our personalities warred from the first, and no subject matter was too trivial to become fuel for controversy. Brick's favorite line of attack centered on my miserable management of Smoky, whom he insisted must be ruled by quirt and spur. Smoky would not, I declared, be touched by either as long as I rode him, so the circumstance became the nucleus of endless feuding. These childish diversions were carried on outside Lydia Sanson's range. One did not misbehave in her presence.

There was a provisional clause to my new teaching contract, written brashly on its margin: "Party of the second part further agrees to supervise manners, morals, and diet of children under her charge from 9:00 a.m. each Monday until the close of school each Friday." I was puzzled, for the phrasing seemed out of character with the general run of country school boards, and I decided it was the idea of a crank director who liked to show off his vocabulary. But I was curious, nonetheless, and wrote asking for an explanation.

An answer came, signed by one Justin MacDeen, stating that I would be met at Rollin Bar on Snake River with a saddle horse and one packhorse to transport my belongings. Not a word about manners, morals, and diet.

I discovered later that an explanation of that detail by "party of the first part" had, in the past, proved unwise. "Party of the second part" usually reacted violently to the proviso and sent back the contract unsigned.

11

Cow Creek Episode

The dance at the Cow Creek School was typical of many we attended that winter and spring. I remember it best because I was directly involved in a fight that night.

Brick was distinctly embarrassed at social gatherings with me on Smoky, and since we were then in one of our romantic phases, I pleased him by riding Dollar, a slender, white-socked bay. Our trail led through rolling hills, greening under April's late afternoon sun. Across Buck Creek divide, we hit a steep trail, best covered in daylight. As the sun sank, a soft wind smelling of moist earth and young growth swept down Cow Creek canyon. Starlight found us still on the trail, and at nine o'clock, we dismounted at the log schoolhouse.

Social life of the river country centered on its schools. In these humble, one-room structures beat the pulse of the people. Emotions came to a focus—humor, pathos, and often savage violence. Desks were pushed back; musicians established themselves on the front platform, food boxes were piled on the teacher's desk, a can on the heater was filled with coffee water, cornmeal was sprinkled on the rough pine floor, and the business of the evening was under way.

Around thirty people had rallied to the call, excluding youngsters, who shouted and took running slides on the floor and tumbled about like young puppies. Two nursing mothers were present. Naturally and unabashedly, they fed their babies. Demanding dance partners had to wait. It was a gay and friendly event. Several of the Wynn riders were there, and one, a tall buck-toothed one, took a special interest in me. Brick, always aggressive, was soon alerted to this development and assumed a lordly proprietorship. He shepherded me away from "Buck Teeth" to a corner for supper and became extremely attentive to my wants.

After supper, dancing resumed. The children, overcome with food and fatigue, were laid out on benches next to the wall and covered with coats or saddle blankets. Most of the men by this time had become flushed and hilarious. The Cow Creek teacher whispered to me that there was a jug of moonshine cached in the huckleberry thicket back of the schoolhouse. The era of tippling ladies had not yet arrived; it was field day for the males. Certain it was that the dance became gayer, noisier, and faster. We danced waltzes and two-steps and circled madly in the Paul Jones. There was yipping and stamping of booted feet. When the circle broke, Brick was there, flushed and bristling, quick to whirl me away from any competitor. This was certainly asking for trouble.

"Buck Teeth" had been hovering around, and finally, in a tag waltz, he became insistent. He was by this time much less than half sober and tagged Brick with a heavy hand. Brick shoved him rudely aside. A remark was made, too low for me to catch, but certainly fighting words as Brick chose to interpret them. In a second's time, the dancers were all drifting toward the door. The musicians laid down their instruments and sauntered out to view the contest while I stood alone in the middle of the floor wondering how the thing had so quickly come about.

The Salmon River dances were not judged really successful affairs without a lusty, barefisted bout or two. Differences were settled in a direct and primitive fashion. It was pleasing to my vanity that two males should be battling over me, but I concluded that Brick's motives certainly could not be attributed to chivalry. He had encouraged the fight because he loved physical combat.

The sounds of violence, grunts, and lusty thumps drifted through the open door. Apprehensive as to the fate of my escort, I went out to join the circle of onlookers. The fray seemed to be in its last stages. Buck Teeth was groggy and reeling, unable to deliver more than an occasional wild haymaker. Brick was jabbing in with short, chopping blows. Finally, one, too fast for me to see, landed vitally, and Buck Teeth collapsed. He was dragged aside from the path and left there to temporary oblivion. We all trooped back into the schoolhouse, and the dance went merrily on. Brick was not marred except for a bruised cheek, but he bore himself with heroic dignity as befitted a champion. Dear Brick, for all his nineteen years, was still a little boy playing at being a hard, tough guy.

A luminous line pinked the eastern sky, dimming the stars. Time for the dance to break up. There were treacherous trail stretches, safer in daylight for babies and womenfolk. The schoolroom looked ugly and desolate in the strengthening dawn. It was a shamble, and I felt sorry for the teacher who was to set it in order for classes. Horses were brought up, and grumpy, sleepy youngsters hoisted aboard. Goodbyes were called, and there was laughter and good-natured ribbing.

We rode off down the trail in the clear, cool dawn. Brick set his gray Stetson at a jaunty angle and whistled a gay little tune. It had been a most satisfactory affair.

12

Vertical Grasslands

In its long sweep from the Bitter Root Range, the Salmon River hews west to its destiny, the Snake. A short distance below Horse Creek Rapids, it enters the great granite mass known as the Idaho Batholith. By furious labor it has worn a canyon deeper at several points than that of the Colorado. Recklessly it plunges through Idaho's great primitive area, only to be thwarted within fifteen miles of its objective and diverted north on a fault zone for more than forty miles. Angrily intent, it surges along parallel to the Snake until again directed west to its union.

After the northward turn, lava becomes the dominant walling of the canyon, sweeping precipitously up to the "breaks." East from these rims lies the gold country, an area of placer and quartz mines. It is a fabulous expanse of misty blue peaks, cut by uncounted canyons. For more than one hundred miles, it tumbles up to the continental divide. Northeast, the Salmon's rims end in a high tableland, which extends to the breaks of the Clearwater. On this flat highland, rich wetlands nurture the towns of Grangeville and Cottonwood. West, in the narrow fork country that separates the Salmon and the

Snake in their parallel flow, lies a portion of Idaho's choice summer grazing. A like land matches it on the Oregon side.

In the early part of the century, homesteaders reduced much of the stockman's public grazing areas, but life on the Salmon River homestead was a precarious existence and had to be supplemented by mining or working for the cattlemen in addition to running a few head of cattle, horses, or sheep. Some of the homesteaders turned to moonshining, in which profits were enticing and risks negligible. In spite of all this, the homesteader's life was a desperate struggle. One by one, they sold out to the big brands. Many left the country; others drifted to the river settlements or the mining camps.

By the late 1920s, most of the homesteaders were gone, and with their departure, the old section line fences fell, disintegrated, and disappeared. Into the new era of big ownership moved the drift fence, which, by aid of cliffs, outcrops, and other features of the terrain, keep cattle in their seasonal range. The winter range is low, on river bars and for some distance up sheltered draws and canyons, as stock can be maintained in fairly good condition with a minimum of feed in low altitude.

The winter range is carefully guarded from encroachment, for the scant hay lands of the bottoms, together with adjacent winter grazing, can mean survival to a herd caught by an unexpected bitter winter.

Fall and spring range extends from winter lowlands up to the rims. These are expanses of near-vertical grasslands, and here the drift fence comes into play, not only to discourage stock from straying back into winter range, but also to prevent them from drifting on northern hillsides during slick weather. Losses from rolling are comparatively light now compared to the old days of careless range practices.

On top is summer range, lush and nutritious, and here the beef crop takes on market pounds. On the plains of the Doumacq and Joseph and on up to the forest reserve lands rolling between the Salmon and the Snake, the river stockmen range their herds. Widespread are their makeshift summer camps. The fall roundup takes tally of the beef with buyers from the metropolitan stock marts present to make their bids.

The old methods of running cattle prevailed largely during my first years in the Salmon River country. The transition was beginning. Slowly it developed into the present-day pattern. Few of the cattlemen of the early days knew how many head they owned. Breeding was haphazard, and calves came at any time of the year. Losses from rolling were high. Many cattle were lost in the fall roundup due to the difficulty of hazing them out of precipitous draws where the brushy bottoms screened them from view. Some of the strays were retrieved by enterprising homesteaders, but most of them died of exposure and starvation when early snows swept the high ranges.

The fortunes of the early cattlemen were unpredictable. So were their methods of business. Nearly everyone was under the heavy hand of the bank. Ranchers could give only an approximate count of their stock; they never knew how many head of cattle they owned. Awareness of worth in dollars was just as hazy. Bankers knew more about a rancher's holdings than he did and frequently advised him in no uncertain terms what he could or could not do. When the beef sold, most of the money went to the bank, to apply on loans. Ultimately it sifted into the coffers of the eastern corporations. In this manner, frontier wealth in cattle, mines, and manpower was siphoned off. In his heart, the stockman knew full well that he was little more than a glorified hired hand, but he still enjoyed prestige in the country where he lived and rode. He made his presence felt among the underling stockmen and those of his own financial stratum. It was a haphazard business, but it did not worry the native cattleman overmuch. Cattle were cheap; he paid little attention to improving his herds. The bank owned everything anyway, so what the hell! The loss of a hundred cattle more or less each year meant nothing to him.

It had its desperate risks, but environment had written his lines, and he was bound to them by the fetters of debt. There was a season of diversion after marketing to be spent in the big western cities or even the packing centers of the middle west. Here he portrayed the role of the big cattleman from the wide, open spaces, and few of his admiring audience guessed the bleak part he, in reality, played. The range country presented its physical hazards, and financial uncertainty was ever with him. But he accepted all with sardonic humor. Everything was "Jake," except when the banker became difficult or when a hard winter decimated his herds.

As the years passed and the really big absentee ownership took over, the grand, old wasteful scale of doing things bowed out. The value of beef took on new significance. A man, or a company, now knows, to the head, how many cattle are owned and where they are at all times. Scrubs are sold off, and care in breeding moves into place. Dehorning and vaccinations are on the books. Breeding is in proper season. No more careless dismissal of strays. No more rolling on slick frozen hillsides. No more slick-ear yearlings and out-of-season calving. Fat young steers, quickly finished off, are big money, and every steer is valuable.

13

Spring and a Young Man's Fancy

"I've enlisted," Brick stated. "In the Navy I'll go places and see lots of action. I'll be called in two weeks."

It was late May 1917 and my last Sunday on the Sanson ranch. My trunk had been shipped home. No more than a pack load of my possessions remained, and Brick was to take me to Rollin Bar next Saturday. After dinner, we rode to a high slope on Round Mountain, which commanded a view of the river road and watched the first motor stage, a REO Speed Wagon, pass on its maiden trip from the rail terminal at New Meadows down the Little Salmon and along the route through White Bird to Grangeville. Many had driven to points along the way to see it pass. Others, like us, watched from high, lonely points its slow and labored progress over the rocky, high-centered road. In spite of delay and the many breakdowns it went through, the feat was hailed with joy by the people of Salmon River, for it marked the dawn of new days and new ways.

For the remainder of that bright spring afternoon, I trailed Brick over the range. We saw the new calves and exclaimed over the beauty of Taffy's colt, a wobbly-kneed, cream-coated confection with fuzzy, white mane and tail.

"Let's name him Candy," I suggested.

"Hell of a name for a man's top saddle horse," Brick snorted. "He'll be about ready to break when I get back."

That a sailor might be required to die for his country did not enter into Brick's calculations. He would return from a short, decisive conflict, resplendent with medals. "A man would do thus and so," he said. He assumed a melancholy dignity to veil the entrancing prospect of release from what he considered the monotony of "this damned river country."

That he might return scarred or maimed or might, indeed, not return at all was unacceptable to his thinking, and I pondered this matter as we rode on. In groups and one by one, the young men were leaving for training camps. For weeks, Brick had talked of little else. His father wanted him to wait for the draft. With what inner conflict Mrs. Sanson accepted the pending separation, I could only guess. She had said, "It's for the boy to decide, Jess." But she seemed thinner and more fragile as time went on, and her deep-set eyes became increasingly somber.

On the ridge of Round Mountain, we drew up. The vast sweep to the river was one of breathless beauty. It was not to be merely looked at as one rode on. I wanted to breathe it, to savor it deeply, to etch it forever on my memory.

"I've got to just look for a while," I said, dismounting.

Obligingly Brick got down, and the mules started to graze, trailing their reins sidewise to avoid trampling them. Mike sat down gratefully and lolled his tongue while we sought the shade of a huge lava outcrop, which offered a magnificent view of the slant to the river. It was a riot of color, with shades of blue and purple predominating. Magenta-hued shooting stars and bluebells, with countless other showy blooms wove a brilliant tapestry at our feet and blended into extravagant washes of lavender on the more distant slopes. I find no words to describe this Salmon River country in the spring. Drenched with a giant paintbrush, its vast remoteness, it's incredible distances, its depth and grandeur are beyond words. Here, war seemed meaningless.

"Do you really want to go?" I asked.

"Of course," said Brick. "A man's got to go. I'll see things— cities and people, ships, and other countries. It'll be great to be free."

So, Brick wanted to be free. If ever a youth were physically free, surely it was Brick. He lounged against the rock, and his whole person was the exponent of freedom. Only his eyes looked somber and intent. *Playing at being a hero,* I thought bitterly. Something lovely went out of the day. Fierce resentment stirred in me that Brick could know adventure, danger, glory perhaps, while I would endure only monotonous days of teaching in drab schools. War, the most diverting and glamorous pastime that man had so far thought up, was denied to me—a woman.

"There's no place with more freedom than you have right here," I said.

"I don't feel free, so I'm not," said Brick with conviction. "I've got to see something beyond these mountains."

"You won't be free in the navy I bet," I retorted. "You'll want to be back here mighty bad."

"Would you want to be back here with me?" he said softly. "After the war, I mean."

"I might be persuaded," I answered, teasing.

Brick then proceeded to demonstrate his brand of persuasion, which I encouraged to a suitable degree and then rebuffed him smartly with the finesse of the proper young lady of that era. It was a technique to suffer ruinously during the approaching 1920s, but it provided a titillating interlude, which matched the tempo of the spring afternoon.

The sinking sun slanted over the western pine-fluted mountains. Deep pools of shadow formed in pockets all over the rugged slope to the Salmon, and a new enchantment of color was displayed. Mike rose, yawned, and stretched. He wagged up to Brick and nudged his arm. When no move was made, he seated himself in front of us and eyed me fixedly. Plainly he intended to get us started home. Brick brought up Smoky and Danny, tightened the cinches, and helped me aboard, pulling my riding skirt neatly to my shoe tops. This little gesture from such a tough guy always amused me. It was a small courtesy, common in this country of riders, of getting a lady safely aboard and in decorous position.

The vogue of riding pants for women had not yet come to the river. Here the divided skirt was the proper attire. Mine was of heavy khaki, worn at shoe-top length, and when I was not in the saddle, it was buttoned primly down the front in an effort to kid myself and the world that it was not constructed for the shocking necessity of straddling a horse.

We rode down the mountain side by side through the sweet spring dusk. In the draw, the syringa bloomed, and its fragrance enveloped us as we forded the creek where the mules stopped to drink. Brick caught my saddle horn, pulling Smoky and me close to him. His lips were eager, his eyes intent.

"You said you could be persuaded," he said huskily. "If I can depend on that, I'll marry you just as soon as I get back."

"Oh, you will!" I exclaimed, enraged at his cool assumption. "And I should be overcome with joy at the honor, I suppose. But I'm not. And I won't be sitting around mournfully waiting for the returning hero either."

"What a damned little snob you are!" There was fury in Brick's voice, and he released my saddle horn with a sudden shove away from him.

"And you are a vain, spoiled brat, trying to be a big toughie," I retorted with equal heat.

He spurred Danny furiously out of the creek, and I let him go, thinking smugly that a stretch in the navy might improve his manners. For reasons that I refused to examine, his rage pleased me, and I rode leisurely across the meadow to the lower gate and then to the barn. Brick unsaddled Danny and turned him into the corral.

"I'll ride Smoky down to the lower pasture. Want to bring in the workhorses," he announced brusquely. I handed him the reins without a word, but a quick glance revealed his eyes, hot blue, and a mean set to his chin.

The next morning, ready for school, I went to the barn for Smoky. I found the poor fellow with sides raked and cut from being spurred, the blood caked and dry on his handsome spring coat. Dreading other disclosures, I looked farther and noted the corners of his mouth were torn from abuse with the bit. He stood there patiently, pathetically. Tears of anger and pity smarted my eyes. With mounting fury, I raged out of the barn back toward the house, determined to find Brick. We met on the path through the orchard

"So," I flared. "Why didn't you beat me last night, since I was the object of your wrath?"

"It would have been a pleasure," he returned with maddening insolence.

"Coward!" I jibed. "To vent your spite on a helpless animal."

"Yeah?" he sneered. "Well he's mine you know, and you've ruined him, letting him have his own way. He needed a working over."

It is better not to record the things I then said to Brick, or the replies he made. But the row was violent enough to bring Lydia Sanson out of the house and down the path.

"Son," she said sternly. "Teacher, what is wrong here?"

We were silent under her steady eyes. Petals from the apple blossoms floated lazily down; the air was rare with their perfume, and the sun laced through in dancing shadows. It was a peaceful and tender setting, and our human ugliness was ill suited to it. Shaking with reaction of my useless rage, I turned silently toward the house. When I returned shortly with a bucket of warm water, soap and salve, Brick was receiving a stern but low-voiced lecture, and I was gratified to note that he looked properly chastened. Down at the barn I washed Smoky's sides and smeared on stock salve, made him a soft bran mash, and rode him that day with a hackamore to save his torn mouth from the bit.

In proportion to the hardships and pain that were, here, the common lot of men and their animals, Smoky's scratches were as nothing. They were fast healing, while the bitterness between Brick and me remained. In my heart, I was sorry and ashamed. He was too, I'm sure, for he carefully groomed Smoky and made his coat shine like gray satin and smartly trimmed his roach. Each morning of those last days, Smoky was saddled waiting for me and was further glorified by Brick's bridle studded with the silver conchas.

14

Day of Days

The last day of the term is a gala event in country schools. On Thursday evening, all was in readiness. The drab little room had been made resplendent with an exhibit of my pupils' accomplishments. Tin cans with frilled crepe paper skirts held a profusion of wild flowers—waxy syringa; shooting stars in purple and lavender; wild roses; delicate, lemon-hued deer tongue; and banks of timberlines. At noon, the mothers would come with a picnic lunch, and a program would polish off the day's activities.

Taking extra time with my appearance the next morning, I was later than usual in arriving at school. As I rounded the last bend in the trail, unusual activity was apparent. There was excited shouting, and my brood dashed about thumping on the building with long sticks. As I rode to the shed to tie Smoky, little Ruth Ann dashed at me shouting, "Teacher, there's a skunk under the schoolhouse."

"Dear Lord," I muttered. "This would have to happen today."

I hurried to the scene, calling to the children to let the skunk alone, that he'd come out finally and go away. They all gathered about me except eleven-year-old Peter, the biggest boy in school that year. Muted thumping was heard from under the building.

"Where's Peter?' I asked resignedly.

"He went under the schoolhouse to drive the skunk out," a small voice informed me.

"Peter, Peter," I called, "come out at once. You'll scare him, and—"

A smothered shout reached us, and a furious bumping ensued. Following came a long silence and a definite odor, not of wildflowers. The odor filled the air and became stronger— violent in its intensity. The youngsters retreated, but I forced myself to advance to the hole in the foundation where Peter had entered.

"Peter," I called anxiously. "Peter."

A retching sob sounded so close that I jumped back, fearful that the skunk might make a dashing exit. But his skunkship had evidently retired smugly to the farthest recess of his hideout, for a moment later, Peter's tragic face peered out at me. Slowly, he wormed himself through the hole. His plight was sad indeed. Dust covered his neat, dark pants; his shirt was a mess. Tears, dirt, and cobwebs made a fantastic design on what had shortly before been a shining morning face. The odor was incredible. It was so violent that it no longer smelled like skunk but was a strangling gas of indeterminate character.

Peter was drenched with it. He lay on the ground and was very sick. The children gathered about at a respectful distance and gazed with awe on their fallen leader.

"Peter," I said gently, "get down to the creek. I'll send Sammy home after clean clothes."

The lad got to his feet and slunk wretchedly to the stream, which flowed through the lower corner of the yard.

The schoolroom reeked. I opened the windows and sadly surveyed our floral and scholastic displays. The place was impossible for a gathering of school patrons, or indeed anyone not equipped with a gas mask. Up the creek a short way was a grassy spot in the shade of cottonwoods. We would have our program there, and it would be a pleasant place for the picnic lunch.

There was undeniably an odor of skunk there too, but the affair went off smoothly enough. Peter's mother arrived and ministered to her son, and the episode was the basis for much joking. But Peter, in spite of his scrubbing and clean clothes, was still quite ill and looked morbidly on the festivities from the shadow of a great rock.

Early in the afternoon, all had departed, and I returned to the schoolroom to stow away the never seen exhibit, dispose of the flowers, and pack my personal belongings. The place still stank dreadfully, and I worked swiftly, cramming into a flour sack my books, papers, clock, pens, pencils, and all the odds and ends one collects in eight months of teaching. The sack was well filled with barely enough slack to tie the open end. I tied my leather jacket on back of the saddle and carried the sack in front. Smoky did not like the huge, bulbous affair and pranced, causing the pens and pencils, which I had in a tin box, to rattle. It took both hands to keep this cargo anchored, so I looped the reins over the saddle horn and let Smoky take his way home.

This was an unfortunate decision, but Smoky had been so docile since Brick "worked him over" that I felt he could be trusted to do the right thing. We were hardly well started however, when he shied at a scurrying chipmunk and gave a jump that nearly unseated me and caused a great rattling in the tin box. Encouraged, he gave a couple of stiff pitches, which landed me in a sitting posture in the path directly ahead of him. My bag likewise landed, burst open, and its contents scattered in all directions. The clock struck a rock and disintegrated, books were strewn about, and papers fluttered off down the mountainside. Smoky pricked his ears and regarded me alertly.

I scrambled up, thankful that no bones were broken, and approached the graceless Smoky. He snorted and leaped up the bank. I clambered after him. He dashed down into the trail and trotted jauntily homeward, the reins still over the saddle horn. *This will teach me*, I thought grimly, *never to trust any living creature again.* I gathered those of my possessions worth salvage and trudged along, a dusty and forlorn figure. Around the next bend, Smoky was poking along. Elated, I hurried toward him. He looked around, threw up his ears, snorted, and broke into a brisk trot.

"Horrible jackass!" I cried, remembering my loving care of his recent wounds.

Again, I sighted him when he stopped to nip grass above the trail. I put down the sack and approached stealthily hoping to take him unaware. He fed until I was almost near enough to touch him. Then without a backward look, he suddenly tossed his head and cantered off. I returned to pick up my sack, reflecting glumly that it was at least three miles on to the ranch. It was useless to try to catch the Smoky mule; he'd keep up this game all the way home. Might as well trudge along and pay no attention to him. This was hard to do, since he managed to keep at an enticing distance just ahead of me. Finally, he stopped and brayed, a feat he performed only in moments of rare elation. This enraged me so that I hurled a rock at him with surprisingly accurate aim, and he hove out of sight at a smart clip.

In places, the trail was deep in dust; otherwise, it was rocky and uneven. I had worn my high-heel shoes that day. My feet ached miserably as I scuffed over the stones. The sun beat down with devilish intensity. Sweat streamed down my face. I smelled like a skunk. I pictured myself limping to the ranch. If only Brick would be somewhere else! I felt crushed by the events of the day. It was too much to be endured—this savage country with its unmanageable animals and uncouth people! What a fool I'd been to sign up for more punishment. Enough was enough. I'd chuck the whole business and go home. That's what I'd do. So engrossed did I become in self-pity that I did not notice the approaching rider until I heard the ring of iron on the stony trail. It would be! Yes, it was Brick, riding Dollar and leading the truant Smoky. He drew up, blocking the trail and gloating over my wretched plight. I stared stonily past him.

"I was riding in from town and saw Smoky hitting it for

home with the reins over the saddle horn, so I figured you'd be along the trail somewhere," he said, grinning hatefully.

In silent distaste, I surveyed him. Laughter was in his eyes. He'd had a fresh haircut and shave. He looked cool and clean and nonchalant, and I hated him for it. He dismounted, took my sack, and drew Smoky up for me to mount.

"Kee-rist!" he exclaimed. "What have you been into? You smell like nothing alive."

This was the knockout blow of the whole wretched day. Grimly I fought back tears. Brick noticed and took my arm gently.

"You're a good kid," he said. "But you're awful dumb. I hate to think what's going to happen when you get into really rough going. Better forget the Hells Canyon deal and go on home. You're sure not the type for *that* country."

A dash of ice water couldn't have been more effective. I drew myself up with what dignity I could command and looked Brick fiercely in the eyes. "Brick Sanson," I said. "You are the most despicable person I have ever known. You are an ill-manned smart aleck, and you've picked on me from the first day I came. But let me tell you this. Neither you nor anyone else will run me out of this country. I'll go when I'm ready, and that's not now. I'm going to Rollin Bar tomorrow, and you're going to take me there, just like you promised."

"All right, alright," he returned with an infuriating grin. "Let's get along. Look now," he added as I climbed into the saddle, "*Keep the reins in your hand.* And keep that damned mule's head up."

15

Cleft of the Snake

Oregon's Wallowa Mountains form the west wall of Hells Canyon. Opposite, on the Idaho side, seven giants of serrate rock thrust torn fingers into the sky more than seven thousand feet above the madly coursing Snake River. These are the Seven Devils, arranged in a semicircle, and their gashed flanks form the east battlement of the canyon.

In the pit of this titanic chasm, forty miles in length, flows the "mad accursed river," growing mightier with every mile as feeder streams plunging through their own long canyons add their force to the formidable water. It falls more than twelve feet to the mile, frequently lashing against visible and hidden barriers of granite. Here the Snake boils in white fury, still gnawing savagely at its channel after having cut a mile through top lava flow and one thousand feet into granite.

It is the continent's deepest chasm and one of many planes rising step like from the river—first granite escarpments giving way to lava walls, with skirts of shale, and then occasional slopes of vagrant cheat grass. Few soft colors fleck its austere wall surfaces. It is dark, forbidding, and so narrow at the highest rims that most of the riverbed lies in constant gloom. Sinister in its splendor, it repels yet fascinates. Its nocturnal hues soften as sunlight strafes the rimrock or shadows from one precipice creep slowly across the opposite wall.

On occasions, the vast cleft seems filled with a thin, blue mist, producing an effect of unreality. The craggy trench with its monstrous rock surfaces softens, becomes nebulous, and loses its cruelty, its melancholy perdurance. In these rare moments, its grandeur is enhanced. It becomes a cosmic masterpiece in tones, a mystery in magnitude.

Occasional bars dot the canyon's course, brave stands of hackberry and chokecherry bushes relieve its austerity, and a sprinkling of ponderosa or yellow pine and other evergreen trees twist their roots into its crevices.

A great land too lies beyond the rims on both the Idaho and Oregon sides. Here, timbered slopes run into areas of national forest and lush summer grazing. Cattle owners and sheepmen vie for grazing privileges, and in earlier days, savage violence marked their strife. The national forest service, keeper of the timber and grasslands, mediates its claims, and though smoldering resentment against regimentation is a characteristic of the native stockman, the national jurisdiction is grudgingly acknowledged and an uneasy truce exists.

Below Hat Point the canyon widens, marking the end of the furious forty miles. The majestic rims give way to steep slopes of evergreen broken by battlements of basalt crags. On this lower stretch, the Snake condescends to permit boat passage, boon to the people who inhabit its bleak bars and creek canyon ranches. Still north at Pittsburg Landing, the slopes are gentler, though nonetheless terrifying in their sheer spread.

Oregon's water, the Imnaha, draining the ancient tribal lands of the Nez Perce, joins the Snake a short distance below the scene of Chief Joseph's epical crossing in the early summer of 1877. Here a great Indian people, harried from their ancestral holdings, moved with all their possessions out into the floodwaters of the Snake by means of rafts lashed at each corner to their powerful Appaloosa horses. Thus, began their fighting trek to the Clearwater, up its rugged Lochsa tributary to Lolo Pass and on to near extinction in battles of the buffalo country.

The confluence of the Salmon marks the merging of two majestic waters, both rapidly falling. It is a welding of magnificent power. The junction of great rivers, incentive to settlements of man, departs from pattern at this wilderness union, and the Salmon maintains its primeval integrity to the last. Few signs of human habitation mark this merging. The waters rush to marriage by the music of their own thunder, which rises with immense reverberations to the lonely grandeur of rigid horizons.

The fury of the Snake abates after it receives its final Oregon water, the Grande Ronde. Between the brown hills of the Lewiston country, it joins its last great tributary, the Clearwater, augmented by the Selway and Lochsa. In maturity, it flows along sedately, with the load of many waters and spent by the turbulence of its raging youth.

The name Hells Canyon was rarely heard in early days, for the people of its country referred to it as Box Canyon or Seven Devil's Gorge, and among the old settlers, there is still reluctance to accept the name by which it is now commonly known. They will tell you this name of Hells Canyon was conferred by those who knew not its "feel." They insist that it does not chord with the canyon's true character, for formidable though it is, it is perfectly attuned to wildlife, providing a barrier to decimation by humankind's ruthless preying. Sturgeon in season abound in the waters of the Snake. Trout flirt in the streams that feed to it through their own impenetrable canyons. Deer and elk find haven in its fastness. For its varied species of wild inhabitants, it is sanctuary, benevolent in its inaccessibility, and for man, with the consciousness to understand and manage his place in nature, there is here a union between the deepest current of human life and its own earth.

The people of the Snake River country, both in Idaho and Oregon, tenaciously guard the water as their own. During past decades, when its forbidding concavity was all too frequently regarded by outsiders as the "jumping off place," they drew themselves to it with the fierce possessiveness of a parent for a disabled child. The trail of cattle and gold dust grows dim as a new potential moves into the scene. Hydroelectric need looms, and attention is focused on the land of America's swiftest waters. Determined to resist the syphoning off of another great resource, its people warily test the currents in the power struggle and prepare for all-out defense.

16

Shanghaied

Jim Garrter had come to Rollin Bar to meet me. For the second time that day, my gear was being loaded on a packhorse. I sat on the bow of the scarred rowboat in which he had ferried me across the Snake and watched as he put a canvas over the pack and then lashed it with a deftly thrown diamond hitch.

"How far is it to—to where we're going?" I asked.

"About five hours to where we top out on the Rim Trail," he said. "Not much climbin' from there on. Ought to make it before dark. Bess'll have supper ready."

"Am I going to stay with you folks?"

"Why no, ma'am. You'll be staying at the school camp with the kids. No outfit is close enough to ride to and from every day."

"The school camp?" I repeated.

"I told Mac he oughta tell you," he said gloomily. Mac then, was the evasive one with whom I'd corresponded.

"He didn't tell me anything," I said.

Jim Garrter observed me soberly as he reached for tobacco sack and papers, leisurely rolling a cigarette. Tall and rangy, he wore a cotton shirt that seemed in danger of not quite meeting the downward pull of leather chaps and heavy cartridge belt. He wore a black vest and battered felt hat. Dark hair rode his collar untidily, giving him a wild look in spite of his clean-shaven face, deeply tanned, with long, tong-like lines from nostrils to the corners of his wide mouth. He had a grim face, except for his dark eyes, steady and trusting.

"They're all good kids," he said at last. "They won't make you trouble. They know to mind, and each one knows to do his or her work at the school camp.

"How many?" I asked faintly.

"Seven in all. Four of ours, and Mac has three."

"Doesn't anyone live close to the school?"

"Our camp's closest, around twelve miles. Unless I'd name Ole Sugar. He's got a shack on Pan Creek, couple of miles from there. But he's kinda daffy. Not bad crazy," he added quickly. "Just plain daffy."

He turned to the saddle horses while I considered the prospect ahead. Marooned in this wilderness for four months with a mob of wild youngsters and a crazy man for a neighbor!

Hopelessly I gazed about me. Except for a decaying log cabin with sunken roof and tumbledown stone fireplace there was no sign that humankind had ever dared to contend with the stark desolation that was Rollin Bar.

Steep slopes rose forbiddingly, shod in vast slides of shale to the river, with an occasional scattering of courageous pine and hackberry. The Snake, slowly clearing, ran wide and rapid. Sullen, grim, it was without reflection. A hundred yards above, rapids tossed angrily. Below, it glided with sinister speed to a rendezvous with midstream crags, which sent white water boiling back in a deafening roar. This was wicked water and beyond the service of the intrepid riverboats from Lewiston. Anxiously, I searched the grim heights on the Idaho side for one last glimpse of Brick, but he was already lost to sight in the rocky vastness.

Looking back on the day I went from the Sanson ranch to Rollin Bar, I recall that, from dawn until early afternoon, we had zigzagged southward to our crossing. Brick led out on Danny, the packhorse followed, and I brought up the rear on Smoky. It was a steep and rock-ribbed trail, fierce with the heat of early summer. We labored in and out of creek canyons, crossed brief wooded slopes, and plodded through rocky passes bristling with serrate segments. Not a sign of human habitation. A grim, self-ravished expanse of torn granite and lava, soundless except for the sullen and distant thunder of the Snake. My spirits descended with the trail. Down and still down we wended our way through crevices and bleak, vertical draws to the river.

At noon, we had ridden steadily for eight hours. Brick judged we were less than an hour from Rollin Bar, so we dismounted at Dice Creek to eat the lunch Mrs. Sanson had put up for us the previous night. Brick loosened the cinches, and the animals drank and nipped bunch grass under the thin shade of aspens.

With great sadness, I stroked Smoky's smooth coat.

I said, "Brick please don't abuse Smoky."

"For cripes sake," said Brick mildly, "will you ever quit loving that old mule?"

"I hate to leave him—and you." The latter admission cost me an effort.

"You would wait until the last minute to say that!" exclaimed Brick, swinging me away from Smoky to face him.

After a while, we got around to eating our lunch, seated at the base of a granite boulder. From this point, a broken vista of the Oregon side was visible. Crag piled on crag in magnificent disorder. Rim after rim of black and gray lava skirted with sweeps of shale, bluff upon bluff of torn basalt. On the highest rims, giant ponderosas and firs were dwarfed by distance to mere shrubs. I was gazing at a small segment of the continent's roughest rock surfaces, terrifying in their desolate grandeur.

Ready to mount the mules, we lingered, I, dreading the finality of this last lap. It was an ill-advised moment for Brick's casual remark: "You'd better watch your step this summer. This is sure enough rattlesnake country."

"I don't want to go on," I cried, wildly swinging away from Smoky. "How can people live in such a place? Please, Brick, let's go back."

"You know you can't," he said gently, catching me and holding me close. "Whoever's meeting you would likely stay all night, and maybe tomorrow, waiting. In this country when a man says he'll do a thing, he does it—a woman, too."

I had minutes of real panic at the parting with Brick, postponing the separation by a barrage of meaningless talk. My belongings were in the boat, and Jim Garrter stood there waiting to shove off. I was afraid to cross the deceptively smooth stretch of water in that frail craft. I was experiencing utter loneliness added to alarm at this dark, wild-looking man with whom I was being left.

Should I demand to be taken back? I dared not voice the thought. Had two men and six beasts struggled for a full day in and out of this inferno to be faced with a change of mind by a terrified girl who was afraid to go on? It could not be done. The very thought implied loss of self-respect. I clutched my remaining shreds of pride and strove to conceal my fright and helplessness, chattering on wildly, trying to keep Brick with me as long as possible.

Sensing my panic, his eyes were remote and miserable, but he dealt with me according to his code. It was the code of a people who do not compromise with weakness. It was the code of their rock—of their river.

"You'd better be getting along," he said and turned casually to rearrange his packing gear.

I searched Jim Garter's face. He stood there at ease, eyes on the river, thumbs hooked over his belt—waiting with patience and determination for this monkey business to be concluded.

"Goodbye," I said miserably, accepting Brick's ultimatum, knowing then there could be no turning back.

"So long," he said shortly, unsteadily. He kept his back turned to me, working swiftly.

But he waited there until we made the crossing—raised his hand in a farewell salute and then turned Danny up the trail, driving Smoky and the packhorse ahead of him.

The canyon was a fierce reverberation of the sun. My face felt blistered. No use sitting there staring helplessly about me. I was, in reality, a captive. There was nothing to do but go on, no alternative but to follow Jim Garrter, to face what was to come and make the best of it. In those moments, I took a long step on the road to maturity.

The saddle horses were beside me. "This is Riley," said Jim Garrter. "He's yours for the summer. I took up the stirrups for you. Step up and see how they suit you."

I stepped up on Riley, a tough little buckskin, wide of chest, with flaxen mane and tail.

"They're fine," I said. "Just the right length."

"Then we'll be digging out of here," he said. "Up a ways, we'll be outa this heat. It's nice at the camp. High and dry up there, but cool."

My eyes lifted to the bleak ramparts of the Oregon side. From the river, the trail led across a meager bar into a crevice between vertical granite cliffs. It was the beginning of a cruel climb, ladder like, through a world of torrid stone. The horses heaved and trembled with the effort. Ahead, the packhorse stepped craftily to avoid scraping his pack against the rock walls. We stopped frequently to "breathe" them. After an hour of stubborn effort, we topped the ridge and dropped into a creek canyon whose walls we were to follow all the way to the final rims.

We made innumerable crossings, sometimes traveling along the stream bed, more often climbing high to avoid sheer cliffs bedded in the creek, still high and swift with snow water. Always on one side or the other was a rock wall with outcropping of shelf like ledges. Jim Garrter's interest seemed concentrated on that wall, and I wondered why. Stupefied with fatigue and heat, I straggled along at the rear of the procession. We crossed the creek again and labored up an incline to a narrow trail along the canyon wall. Jim Garrter still rode with that listening, watchful turn of the head.

I did not see his gun withdrawn—saw only the frantic movement of the horses ahead and heard two quick shots, explosive in the boxlike canyon. Jim's horse reared and plunged, rocking the pack animal into the wall and back to the edge of the trail. One leg went over and I watched fascinated as he tried to gain footing. The momentum of the pack was too much. He plunged over the cliff, landing on his back between two boulders, which caught the pack and held him there, legs thrashing futilely.

Concern for the fate of my belongings vanished as Riley,

catching the terror of the other beast, sidestepped, crushing my right leg against the jagged rock and scraping it cruelly. When I could look again, Jim Garrter was already down in the boulders and had managed to separate packsaddle from horse. With dexterous use of the hackamore, he succeeded in getting the beast on his feet. The horse tossed his head, shook himself, and nonchalantly cropped a tuft of grass beside the rock.

Jim looked up, seeming not much perturbed. "You all right?" he called.

I said that I was, not mentioning my leg, which I thought surely broken. The man had trouble enough.

"One rattler less," commented Jim, "but he almost got me."

I urged the reluctant Riley forward to view the remains. The rattlesnake, a huge fellow, had been poised in a tight coil on the ledge just even with the saddle cantle when Jim's bullets pierced the coils in a dozen places. The reptile's impressive length, ragged and torn, lolled across the ledge, and the hideous head hung by a segment over its edge. I turned away sickened, but not before I counted his fourteen buttons.

"Sure messed up your gear," Jim remarked, handling the shattered cartons of my pack.

It took time to repair the packing gear and reload. I sat miserably on the drowsing Riley, and the pain in my leg mounted with the passing moments. I dared not dismount for fear that I would have to be helped back into the saddle. Mixed with physical torment was shame that I wasn't watching my business in a tight place. There were ways of avoiding that grinding impact. Brick would have expressed deep disgust at my carelessness, and I was pretty sure Jim Garrter was of the same school. There was no immediate help for my injury that I knew. I wriggled my toes tentatively and the effort sent slivers of pain surging to my hip.

The task of getting the packhorse back on the trail consumed more time. When we were ready to start, Jim unfastened a roll carried behind his saddle and handed me a strip of jerky.

"In case you get hungry," he remarked. "It'll be night now before we top out."

"Are there rattlesnakes at the school camp?" I asked dully.

"Nope," he assured me. "It's too cold up there. They like it hot."

By the time we were on our way again, the canyon lay in deep shadow. We had lost a lot of time. I missed Smoky's smooth gait. Riley was a rough traveler, and as he jogged on the increasing smooth sections of trail, I felt faint with pain and general wretchedness, no longer caring where I was going or what the next few months held for me. The horror of a coiled rattler striking my face or shoulder from a ledge in the wall even faded to passivity.

Darkness came, heavy and close with the heat stored in the rock walls. A scant strip of sky sprinkled with stars told me that we were still deep in the creek canyon. We moved through a black void punctuated only by the ring of shod hooves against stone and the roar of the water below. Jim Garrter called back to me frequently. With effort, I masked my misery with an assuring answer. As time passed and we climbed steadily, the thrash of water became fainter. Laboring toward widening starlight, the blackness softened to deep gloom. If we did not "top out" soon, I felt surely that I would tumble from the saddle and lie prone in the trail. To lie anywhere, anyhow, for even a few minutes, would be a respite supreme.

Hunger added to my wretchedness, and I extracted the strip of jerky from my shirt pocket. It was of the texture of wood and just as hard, but I gnawed it and tried to remember when I had last eaten a meal. The hurried breakfast we had consumed in the Sanson kitchen seemed an episode of some period long ago. It could not have been in the dawn of this day I'd lived.

At last the heavens widened, seeming very near and heavy with stars. A vast space yawned at our left. We were on top. On the Rim Trail at last. Our way became smooth and wider. Jim Garrter's horse set out at a swift, swinging walk. Riley jogged. I rode my stirrups and was relieved to find that my leg bore the weight well enough—*not broken at least.* I brightened somewhat at the thought in the cool reviving air after the close swelter of the canyon.

It was more than cool in that lean altitude. June though it was, there was frost in the air, and it lanced through my thin shirt, damp with perspiration of the past hours. Soon I was shivering and thoroughly cold, but rather than endure the pain of twisting in the saddle to unfasten my jacket tied behind, I rode on, knowing the end must now be near.

A duet of barking heralded our approach to the school camp. My confused senses took in a lantern swinging from the ridgepole in front of a tent and a tall woman striding like a man to meet us.

"You're late," she announced. "Musta had trouble. You all right, teacher?"

I said that I was and attempted to swing off my saddle with a show of agility, but meeting the earth, I buckled and would have fallen but for her strong arm, which steadied me and propelled me toward the tent.

17

High and Dry

Where the Rim Trail dipped into a gully, a wide place accommodated a huddle of canvas and rough lumber shelters strongly resembling a ragged Indian camp. Under a group of majestic ponderosas were three tents stretched over pole frames, each with a rough floor of boards. The largest was the cook tent; the other two set back from the trail were sleeping quarters. A hundred feet above was a spring and water troughs for the horses. Following the gully down toward the canyon rim was a stout corral of lodge pole pine.

The nucleus of this wide place in the trail was the schoolhouse, small and square with a steep peaked roof. It was sturdily built of tough fir and sat firmly on its log foundation, further anchored by two cables snubbed about great lava outcrops. By such means, it had managed to survive the terrific gales, which, in winter, sweep the breaks of Hells Canyon.

Thus, on the ragged flanks of the Wallowa's stood this strange center of learning in the wilderness. This was the school camp; this was "manners, morals, and diet."

It approached midnight when we ate supper the night of my arrival, a plain meal of boiled potatoes; steak; a heavy, white gravy made with condensed milk; light bread; and stewed dried peaches.

Bess Garrter was apologetic. "We'll have better grub," she said "soon's the river gardens get in bearing. We'll have you fresh stuff every week. Pack it up from the river."

I studied the gaunt woman seated beside me on the bench at the plank-topped table. Big boned and angular, her face was a bleak pattern of toil. Not young, not old—her age was unguessable. The reflection of far distances lay in her eyes. Tawny hair coiled carelessly at her neck, escaped in wisps like frayed rope ends. I felt an immense respect for her capability. Those strong, big-knuckled hands had treated my injury with tenderness and decision. And I was immeasurably relieved at her nonchalance as to its seriousness, though the knee was swollen, and to walk was pure pain.

Jim Garrter was gravely concerned when told of it. "We'd better try to get her to a doctor," he said immediately.

"'Tain't that bad," his wife replied quickly, "just a bone bruise. A few days, and it'll be all right. The younguns will be here Monday morning, and I'll stay a few days until that swellin' goes down."

Jim, however, was not convinced and discussed means of getting me "outside." There were, it developed, three marked means of exit from the rim country, other than the one we had traveled that day. One was south along the Rim Trail to Homestead and, eventually, Huntington. It involved strenuous riding in and out of deep creek canyons, which broke the rims all the way to the southern escarpments of the canyon. Another was a canyon trail, harsh as the way from Rolling Bar, leading from the Garrter's summer camp down to their home ranch on Snake River. There, once a week, the boat from Lewiston left supplies and picked up outgoing letters and passengers. The third route lay across the Wallowa Mountains, in and out of the rugged gorges of the Imnaha and Big and Little Sheep creeks along the trail on which beef were driven to shipping points at Joseph or Enterprise.

Any of the three involved at least two days in the saddle over treacherous trails I had come to know only too well, plus other methods of primitive travel, to reach any town of moderate size. While presenting an honorable method of escape, the memory of the past eighteen hours was so vivid that I was prompted to interrupt Jim's probing of possibilities.

"I'd rather not," I said. "Mrs. Garrter says there's no bone broken, and if she'll stay with me a few days ..." I trailed off weakly and swallowed several times.

Bess Garrter's eyes were on me in quick concern, and she rose at once and began removing tableware.

Jim plunged into an explanation of the school camp setup, which through previous summers had developed into a system, and under the cover of their combined effort to distract me, I got myself under control. I was determined not to break down at this stage of the game.

My duties were to teach the school and see that the mechanics of group living were carried out in a creditable manner. Each child had his or her chores to do, and it was for me to see that they were done. There were to be no rewards for successes, in school or out, Jim Garrter warned me solemnly, only punishment for tasks unperformed.

"And anything you don't care to take on, me and MacDeen will handle when the kids come home Friday night," he concluded ominously.

He made a list of the camp duties of each of my charges, a straight program of work. It looked like a tough assignment, especially for the children, and I said so.

"For eight months a year, they're footloose," Jim explained. "So, they can stand to be fenced in for the other four. Besides, they take to it. Can't hardly wait for school to start.

"We'd like it if they could learn to read better," he continued, and his dark eyes where wistful. "Seems like only four months of schoolin' don't amount to much. I always figure if you can read—and want to read—you can somehow learn yourself. And if any of our kids showed they could use more schoolin', we'd find a way to send them down to Lewiston to regular school. If you could just learn them to read good this term, maybe the next teacher could work on their 'rithmetic. Mac and me agreed to put it up to you."

He regarded me hopefully.

"The course of study, ---" I began, recalling my briefing in this sacred prerogative of the state.

"Won't nobody be checkin' on you," he interrupted. "No

county superintendent has ever visited the school camp yet, and I don't reckon one ever will get enough nerve to tackle it." He smiled grimly.

"This dee-strict's pore," Bess Garrter broke in. "Most of it bein' in the forest reserve, it don't assess up to much, so we pay all we kin from our school tax and makeup the rest out of our own pockets. We know it's hard on the schoolma'am, but," she added, "your board won't cost you a cent, and me and Miss Mac does your laundry and mendin'."

"I'll teach them to read the best I can," I said with swift concern for their starkly outlined need—the desperate toil involved in setting up and maintaining this school, their hopes for four short months of "schoolin'." Under the stimulation of food, warmth, and relaxation, coupled with their evident concern for my comfort and welfare, I even felt a slight enthusiasm for this outrageous assignment.

"Jim, you got to get rid of that Maxie," Bess remarked suddenly. "Since he got that foot smashed last winter, he's no account for work, and he never gets enough to eat. Other dogs gyp him out. I got no time to feed him special. He's getting thin as a rail."

At the sound of his name, a diminutive shepherd dog with silky black coat and the familiar tan markings appeared in the door of the tent, entered hesitatingly, and surveyed us with anxious eyes. His right foreleg was no more than a stump at the paw.

"Yeah," agreed Jim, "he tries to work, but with three legs, he holds us up. He was the best stock dog of the lot, and the smartest. I'll shoot him tomorrow on the way back to camp." He sighed heavily.

At this, the plumed tail ceased to wag, the alert ears fell. Maxie stood motionless, crippled forefoot held delicately aloft.

"Purty smart, pore little feller," said Bess. "Knows what we're talking about all right.

I stretched out my hand to the condemned dog, and he limped to me, rested his head in my lap. His soft, brown eyes explored my face with a desperate yearning. There was the slightest hopeful tail wag.

A late moon had arisen and the open tent flaps framed black shadows of the ponderosas on the pale dust of the trail. A thin sheen of frost gleamed on the corral poles down the draw. I could distinguish Riley's silver mane among the closely bunched blacks and bays of the saddle and pack animals. Farther down, across the rim, a wraith of mist hung over the great abyss of the Snake, and above it, the snow-filled ravines of the towering Seven Devils gleamed like silver lances. Under the cold, white light, the silence was cosmic.

The sharp chill penetrated the cook tent in spite of the camp stove that Bess Garrter kept well stocked with wood. A confusion of supplies was stacked almost to the ridgepole of the tent—staple groceries, bedding, utensils, and the various accoutrements of camp life.

"Those guns," I remarked, indicating two rifles propped against cases of condensed milk. "Are they to be left here?"

"Yes," Jim said flatly. "Always loaded and always in easy reach. These kids know when to handle guns and when not to. You never know when you'll need one— bad."

I offered no further protest.

Later, in my bunk in the girl's tent, I lay motionless. Bess Garrter's breathing in the opposite bunk indicated deep slumber. In spite of the most fatiguing day I had ever known, sleep denied me. My temporary lift of spirits sank again into a channel of misery. Sternly I told myself that I was nearly eighteen, grownup surely; that I had been offered a way out and had refused it; that I had signed a contract and must live up to it; and that I was too soft to take it, just as Brick had said.

Unable to lash myself out of the tormenting groove of self-pity and succumbing to fatigue and the pain in my throbbing knee, I wept softly in despair and loneliness, choking back sobs that might awaken Bess.

But other more alert ears had heard. A shadow etched the triangle of moonlight on the plank floor, and Maxie entered and limped toward me. My hand went out to him, and his forelegs were up on the bunk, his velvet muzzle against my wet cheek. The plight of this small, crippled creature diverted attention from my own woes. Knowing that Jim Garrter planned to leave before dawn with the pack train to be back in his camp to direct the next week's work and make ready their children for the school camp, I was suddenly determined that Maxie should not be available to start on what was to be his last trek.

"Maxie," I whispered. "They're not going to shoot you. They're not. You're mine, Maxie. Mine."

Instantly, he was on the bunk at my side, snuggled close against me. His nearness, his warmth comforted me, and I slept.

18

Manners, Morals, and Diet

It was midmorning Sunday when I awoke, unable at first to comprehend the gently undulating canvas above me, flecked with moving shadows of the ponderosa. A soft breeze tugged at the tied tent flaps and spoke soothingly in the tops of the sentinel pines. The sharp, dusty drench of their needles was all about me. Replacing the night's chill was an invigorating, dry warmth.

Bess Garrter's bunk was neatly spread up, but I was by no means alone, for Maxie lay at my side, muzzle on paw, studying me intently. From that moment through my four months at the school camp, I was never without Maxie. By unspoken agreement, Maxie was accepted as part of my scant accouterment. Where I slept, there slept Maxie; at school, he sentineled the door or drowsed under my desk; at meal time, he was as close to the cook tent door as was permitted; and when I traveled, he was at Riley's side. The brief doggy excursions he permitted himself were always undertaken with an eye to my whereabouts, and at the end of my Hells Canyon sojourn, he rode the white water with me to Lewiston, guarded my luggage during the two-day train ride to Boise, and there accepted the comforts of suburbia with philosophic dignity.

So stiff and sore in every muscle that the injured knee ran a second in competition for my attention, I nonetheless dressed hurriedly and hobbled down to the cook tent. I was refreshed by sleep, and in the bracing air of the high altitude, the resilient spirit of youth asserted itself. The wretched trek of the preceding day was already a remote thing. Glad again to be alive, I was ravenously hungry. I breakfasted alone on cold biscuits, bacon, and stewed peaches, saving a portion of my bread and bacon for Maxie, together with part of the white gravy left from the evening meal.

Gone was the disorder of the night before. Bedding had disappeared. Canned goods and other foods were arranged neatly in improvised cupboards of stacked packing cases; trivets and kettles hung from nails beside the stove; water bucket, washbasins, and towels were arranged on a bench just inside the door.

Thumping sounds from the schoolhouse indicated the center of activity, and thither I made my way to find Bess Garrter pulling down a pack rat nest from the attic, a sodden and odoriferous mess that dripped nastily through wide cracks in the ceiling. Hearing me below, she clambered down.

"Them danged rats," she observed, her tawny mane disheveled and hanging down in her eyes. "Every winter they set up in this attic. I gotta scrub this place from top to bottom, but first off, I want have a look at that knee. I fixed up a herb poultice this mornin'. We'll just slap that on. Learned it from an old Nez Perce squaw. It's done the job many's the time, and it'll do it agin."

Down in the cook tent, she surveyed my disfigured limb, now an ugly blue from calf to thigh, further enhanced with bulbous knee. She slapped on the poultice, an evil-looking mess, green-gray in color, with a peculiar stench, bitter and nauseating, binding it on with strips of worn muslin.

Thus encased, I followed her back to the school, gathered records, and returned to work at the cook tent table. Here I laid out an overall campaign for four months of intensive attack on the mother tongue, studied the school register for a preliminary survey of my seven charges, and composed a glib and lying letter to my mother describing my pleasant quarters in the summer home of a cattle baron. As an extra embellishment, I transformed the stolid Riley to a handsome palomino, which I would ride to school each day or, on suitable occasions, canter down to the boat landing to pick up mail left by the Lewiston boat. My mother must not know, must never know, how my present situation surpassed her wildest apprehensions of "that wild Salmon River country."

A wash basin bath in the girl's tent and the unpacking of my shattered belongings completed the early afternoon's activities. The airy frocks I had brought for my summer school sojourn were here an absurdity. I laughed aloud at the high-heeled footwear, so hopefully packed, and was moved to further merriment at sight of the crumpled Italian straw with floppy brim and wreath of mangled daisies. What I now needed, and badly, was another stout riding skirt, boots, and a supply of long-tailed blouses. The tailored tricotine suit that graced my first appearance on the Salmon River and had been little seen since, was packed reverently away, accompanied by the hope that it might present a creditable appearance "outside" at the end of my four month's incarceration.

"Only thing you need to do outside school," Bess Garrter informed me as she prepared our late dinner, "is decide on each day's grub and see to the cuttin' of the meat." Slicing steaks from a large chunk of beef, she continued, "You won't lose no meat if you keep it sacked close and slung high." To illustrate this point, she slipped the hunk back in a stout muslin sack, tied the end securely, and hoisted it high by means of a rope flung over a branch of the ponderosa.

"Me and Mis Mac bake up light bread for the school camp every week, so's the main thing is to make out the day's grub list and see them two girls cook it right and serve it decent."

"Them two girls," it developed, were her own Essie, barely eleven, and Maryadee MacDeen, one year her senior. Both, she insisted, could "cook good when they'd a mind to."

"Our Young Jim," she told me proudly, "will be your big help at the school camp. Bein' our oldest, he's always taken the brunt of things. He's a sight like his pa, always ready to do for folks. Him and Clem, that's MacDeen's oldest, do a good job alookin' after the horses, packin' and keepin' the gear in order, gettin' out wood too, if it's too much for the little fellers."

"There's another MacDeen child," I said consulting the school register.

"Little Johnnie," she broke in. "Same age's our Eulie. Neither of them topped out enough to know if they're goin' to be much account. But they can carry wood and water and help keep the camp picked up and clean.

"What about Bib?" I asked again, scanning the official list. "Bib Garrter. Is that his real name?"

"His name's Alfred," stated Bess. "But he don't come to it, so we call him Bib 'cause he's always rippin' the bib offen his overalls. Don't take to bib overalls like the other younguns. He's a sight of a boy, that Bib. Lively as a colt and smart as a whip. That's why Jim gives him plenty to do at the school camp."

Going over the duty list, I saw that Bib had indeed drawn a full program. For him was reserved the janitor duties at the school, daily cleaning and liming of the toilet, garbage disposal, together with all-out cleanliness of the grounds. Bib had enough to keep two boys busy, but such precautions did not deter him from other highly disturbing activities, as I was to later learn.

Returning to my strategic planning, I decided that the presence of Bess in the school camp did not present a likely start for the term's work. It might be interpreted by the children as weakness or uncertainty on my part. I had better get going the first day under my own steam, and accordingly, when Bess treated my knee and changed the poultice that evening, I told her about it.

"'Twould be better," she agreed. "That swelling's gone down already. And the Lord knows I've got enough to do at the camp, cleanin' up the mess a passel a men makes tryin' to cook for themselves, besides washin', bakin', and makin' a pack trip to the river ranch. I'll just light out'n here in the mornin' before the younguns come. That'll leave you to do things your own way."

Her horse saddled the next morning and ready to go, she lingered to admonish me as to the use of the herb poultice and warned against being much on my feet.

"You'll come home with the younguns Friday evening," she said in parting and turned her horse up the trail north to the Garrter camp, riding with the unconscious grace of a long-limbed man.

With increasing uneasiness, I awaited the arrival of the Garrter-MacDeen fry, feeling that much of the success of this peculiar arrangement depended on impressions of the first day, and as the minutes passed I began to fight a sort of wild panic. Maxie, feeling my tension, whined softly and gazed expectantly along the north trail. He heard the approaching cavalcade long before I did and, in a hoarse bark ill-suited to his small dimensions, apprised me of its coming. Soon the procession streamed into camp—five saddle horses, two carrying double, two heavily loaded packhorses, and two dogs. With proper dignity, I greeted each child by name, thankful for the briefing given me by Bess Garrter.

Young Jim, a slim, dark lad with his father's steady eyes, aided by fattish Clem of the MacDeen clan, proceeded to the task of unpacking and caring for the horses with occasional shy glances toward me. I felt the covert scrutiny of Maryadee's alert, dark eyes as she extracted her belongings from the packs, accompanied by bossy orders to Essie, a shy, awkward child with flaxen hair braided in tight pigtails. Miss Maryadee MacDeen, I decided, should be put in her place this first day.

The two little boys were indeed far from being "topped out," and after an interval of regarding me questioningly, they were off like lively chipmunks to various spots held dear by association of the previous summer.

The only one of the seven who examined me with unabashed candor, accompanied by a series of wide grins, was Bib. From his thatch of blond hair, alert eyes of deepest blue, and freckle-laced nose to the amazing details of his costume, he was indeed, as Bess had said, "a sight of a boy." Scorning the neat bib overalls of his contemporaries, he wore a conglomeration of cast-off riding regalia; boots much too large for him were set off by waist-length overalls rolled at the cuffs to display the ancient but fancy stitching of the boot tops. His only concession to the normal was a blue cotton shirt, which he was continually stuffing under his waistband, the latter graced with a wide leather belt. On occasions, he spat handsomely through his teeth.

It was his hat that compelled my fascinated gaze—a scarred gray Stetson of great girth rode his ears, spreading them wide and giving his face a distinct gargoylish cast. It was brim-rolled in a nonchalant V, adorned with a band of rattlesnake skin, and its crowning glory was an additional band of rattles in varying lengths fastened in a tight row above the repellent band. They rustled with an almost hissing sound when he moved. Later I was to learn that there were forty-four of the sinister trinkets, and Bib had a story for every one of them. He was altogether as fearsome an example of the ten-year old American urchin as has ever been portrayed by brushstroke or pen.

Precisely at nine o'clock, I rang the little hand bell. Schoolin', plus "manners, morals, and diet" was off to a flying start.

19

The Summer Camp

Friday afternoons were anticipated with pleasure at the school camp, for they marked the weekend trip home and meant baths, clean clothes, a fresh supply of food, and mail. The latter was stale by the time it reached me, for it came up on the boat from Lewiston, was dropped off along with staple supplies at the river ranch, and made the last leg of the trip by pack train to the summer camp. It was mail, nonetheless, and now my only link with the outside world. That, with the simple comforts and adult companionship of the summer camp, made Friday a day of consequence.

Early in the afternoon, Young Jim and Clem rounded up the horses, saddled them, and packed the articles to be returned to the summer camps. Soiled clothes and towels went into one pack with the cans for kerosene. The others carried containers for food. All were packed in cases that had originally held two five-gallon cans of kerosene. Everywhere throughout the river country these boxes were used in such manner, reinforced when necessary, and did service until they disintegrated.

At dismissal of school, the tempo of activity stepped up. Horses were saddled ready to go; the last hitches were thrown on packs. Foods that might attract bears, together with the guns, were stored and locked in the schoolhouse. The younger children scampered about gathering treasures of schoolwork or collections of objects gathered about the camp to be taken home for display. By four o'clock, we were off. Clem led out with Young Jim. The rest of us straggled out along the trail. I rode in the rear, keeping the young children always in sight. The dogs took up their usual scouting positions—Jupe well in the lead of the procession, Tiny ranging from one side to the other and up and down the length of the cavalcade, and Maxie behind me. This weekly parade always took the same pattern, and other than the usual jockeying for position by the younger children, it was an orderly trek. Uneventful, except that the horses after five days of idleness were inclined to shy at imagined terrors along the trail, and Clem, who like to show off in full view of the troupe, teased his horse and frequently got himself bucked off.

The Rim Trail was cut by three canyons between the school and the summer camps. We angled down into the deep shadow of Race Creek, which had hewn its bed from solid lava. Its sides rose in perpendicular cliffs, and our way ran like a thread along its walls. So narrow was it that our packs were built high to prevent possible snagging on the outcrops. Threshing in its boulder-strewn bed, Race Creek carried a sizable volume of water even in summer, but during flood season, it became a formidable creek, and fording at this point was not attempted. Instead, a detour led upward to a narrower section, where a bridge consisting of two logs had been thrown across the torrent. During my stay, we were never forced to make this long and arduous detour except once when a heavy August rain swelled the stream to the danger point. I was always apprehensive on this section of the trail, fearing that a misstep on that narrow shelf might send a pack animal or horsed rider hurtling down the precipice. We always paused at the ford, where we allowed the horses to drink and frequently dismounted to gather fern or flowers that grew luxuriantly in the deep shade. The climb out offered more security because of frequent outcrops that fenced the trail from the drop-off.

There was smooth going to Ladder Creek, a less formidable cut with a friendlier trail and at the bottom a series of ladder like falls that slid over ledges in the creek bed.

Last, at Squaw Creek, the trail forked, and here the MacDeens took a steep way that followed the canyon wall to a high meadow where their camp was located. It was here that Maxie got aboard and rode the rest of the way in front on my saddle, for after eight miles of stony going, his progress became painful. On three feet, his pads became quickly bruised, so I reached down and hauled him up before me, the placid Riley accepting this additional passenger without protest. In time, it became Maxie's custom to run ahead at this point and scramble with great effort to the top of a lava block that skirted the trail. There he waited for us, tail wagging furiously, anticipating the short jump from his perch to my saddle. Frequently, he barked impatiently in an attempt to hurry us along.

From Squaw Creek to the Garrter camp, the trail was smooth and not steep. The last lap was made in less than an hour. If we refrained from dawdling along the trail, which we frequently did, the overall time was about four hours from school to the Garrter camp.

Custom decreed that the teacher takes turns at the Garrter and MacDeen camps, but I preferred the Garrter camp and found every excuse to spend my weekends there. Toward Justin MacDeen, ponderous, florid, and untidy, I continued to nurse a grudge for the mean trick he had played during the period of our correspondence. I had set myself doggedly to endure the routine of school camp, and before the end of the summer, I even found myself enjoying life on the rims. But to the last, I resented Justin MacDeen's frequent recital of his perennial cunning in snaring teachers and took with ill grace his good-humored heckling about being shanghaied.

Mrs. Mac, as she was known throughout the high range country, was a fusser. The MacDeen camp was as neat as a pin, and why her passion for order and cleanliness did not extend to the person of her big husband I was never able to determine. She was also adept at supervising the affairs of others. My sojourns in their camp were periods of cross-examinations as to my past, present, and future, and I felt myself under scrutiny every minute of my stay. Pleading that riding the additional miles to their camp put an extra strain on my slowly mending leg, which indeed it did, I finally gravitated to permanent weekending with the Garrter's.

The Garrter's summer cattle camp was similar to other high meadow camps. The main building was about forty feet long, built of logs with a steep roof covered with shakes.

Unsealed, every detail of its massive structure was visible, for it was intended to withstand gales and the weight of deep snow. The shakes, curled at the edges, emitted light, for the main room was without windows. Actually, its roof covered three sections—the big room, an open breezeway, and the cookhouse, which boasted windows covered with mosquito netting and a door with a wire screen. The breezeway between the big room and the cookhouse was the favored section for congregating during the long summer evenings. Here a pipe from the spring poured water into a wooden trough carved from a tree trunk. Wash basins and coarse towels occupied their places along one bench, and the end walls were adorned with hanging tubs and washboards. There were additional benches and enormous chopping blocks, all favored for lounging as endless talk of the range flowed on, interspersed with rough banter and horseplay.

The big room was furnished with a table, several chairs with laced rawhide seats, and a lounge made of boxes and boards with a bedroll spread on top. The rest of the room was given over to storage—stock salt, cases of canned goods, ropes, canvas, pack outfits, bridles, extra saddles, chaps, boots, and blankets. All were scattered about in disarray or hung from wooden pegs fitted into the rough log walls. There were no barns at the summer camps, only corrals, so the big room did double duty.

Occasionally, we had Saturday night dances there, shoving supplies back in a corner and dancing to the music of Jim Garrter's fiddle and sometimes a guest harmonica. On such occasions, the MacDeens came, together with various unattached riders and Dean and Donna Trelschmeir, twin brother and sister from the Trelschmeir camp to the north.

They were a handsome pair, these twins, and their father's brand graced more cattle than all the other outfits combined. These social episodes lasted until dawn. Often, I rode with the young Trelschmeirs to their camp for Sunday breakfast, and Pat Garrter, a young man of considerable charm, rode with me.

Always, friendly disorder prevailed at the Garrter camp, which was notable for its fluid population. Situated just off the Rim Trail and sheltered by hundred-foot ponderosas, it was a handy stopping place. It was not uncommon for its long cookhouse table, seating twelve, to be filled to capacity for breakfasts and suppers with an overflow awaiting the second table.

Mrs. Mac had not approved of the camaraderie of her neighbor's camp.

"No wonder those Lewiston bankers own Jim Garrter lock, stock, and barrel," she confided with what seemed to me considerable relish. "They feed the whole country. Bess getting meals for every rowdy who happens along, besides making a pack trip to the river at least once a week. Slaving herself to the grave. And Jim's no manager. Hiring four riders all the range season besides a man and his wife at the river ranch. Could do with half that many, to say nothing of the drifters who happen along, looking for a place to throw their saddles."

"Jim can't resist a poker game either," she concluded with satisfaction. "You can't pay off mortgages with that kind of business."

20

Men of the Fading Frontier

With the Garrter's, fare was plain and comforts meager, but openhearted friendliness prevailed. My first activity on arrival at dusk Friday was a warm bath in a washtub in Bess Garrter's quarters, a windowless log cabin with a canvas hung over the door for privacy. Bess had my water heated in five-gallon kerosene cans on her cook stove. My clothes, laundered and repaired, awaited me. I slept in a lean-to room off the Garrter's cabin, and it was reserved for me alone, a matter for which I was duly grateful. Its bed was like those at the school, a pole frame laced with rawhide and topped with a ticking stuffed with moss and pine needles, but it was made up with unbleached muslin sheets, a luxurious accessory compared to the coarse blankets at the school camp.

Bess and I visited over a late supper, kept warm for me in the oven. Often it was highlighted by some delicacy, a little pat of butter or a piece of cake made with eggs, for such perishable commodities were almost unknown at the summer camps. The ordinary camp cake, and one that we frequently baked at school, was made by boiling a mixture of sugar, water, raisins, bear grease, spices and salt and, when cool, adding flour and soda.

Many of my profession complained of their obscure role in the life of their communities, but I occupied rather a special place in the camp country. My food and bed, such as it was, my laundry, and my saddle horse all went with the job. All were freely bestowed, and all were the best that the outfits had to offer. I had the feel of belonging yet was accorded a special deference for my supposed superiority in the realm of "schooling." Of my seventy-dollar-a-month salary, which was tops in country schools at that time, I had the entire amount when I left. There were no deductions and no means of spending it but by mail order. I was restrained from ordering nonessentials through memory of the horse-killing trails from Snake River to the rims.

Other than the family and Pat Garrter, Jim's nephew, there were the men who either rode for or ranged their cattle with his, generally making the Garrter camp their headquarters. They were a fair cross section of the men of America's vanishing frontier.

Bantam-sized Estie Raber was rustically clad and moved with a strange gait. Estie had worked with cattle all his life, but now, crowding middle age, he was still striving to count his first one hundred head. He was ever garrulous, discussing at length his home place on Chance Creek, the scant possibilities it afforded for wintering more than a few head of stock, along with animated references to "deals" always about to be closed, which would expand his holdings and create a miracle herd.

Estie's conversation was interspersed by references to Allie and the kids. Allie was wonderful, staying down there on that canyon ranch all through the hot summers, raising a garden, and putting by what she could for winter.

"Why just think," he was wont to exclaim, "ten years ago, I was just a fiddle-footed cowhand. And now! Now I've got Allie and the kids—six of 'em. Greatest day of my life when I walked into that Lewiston eatment place, and there was Allie, just waitin' to wait on me. A fine young gal like Allie goin' for an old, busted-up cowhand like me! And those kids! Yes, sir, six of 'em. Just like that!" He snapped his fingers, and I had visions of lush litters of guinea pigs appearing miraculously from nowhere.

During such recitals, he was observed contemptuously by Dace Bolter, younger of the two Bolter boys who ranged cattle in considerable numbers. Dace, in his mid-thirties, was tall, lean, and insolently deliberate in speech and movement. Woman trouble had left him with a dim and embittered view of the fair sex. Some six years ago, he had brought an attractive blond bride to the country, but at the conclusion of one round of summer camping and a winter on their isolated bar ranch on the Snake, she had taken the boat for Lewiston one day and failed ever to return. Dace had attempted no known reconciliation, and his marital status was still a subject of conjecture. He enlightened no one but was diligent in cultivating the role of woman-hater among his contemporaries.

Mrs. Mac, to whom all things personally scandalous were known, informed me blandly that Dace Bolter was a scamp, leaving his bachelor brother, Dave, to the mean chore of feeding cattle at the home ranch while he spent the winter season in riotous living in Spokane, making merry with "fast" women, drinking, and gambling.

"Woman-hater, bah!" Mrs. Mac scoffed. "Don't hate 'em so bad but that he hangs around for Bess Garrter's good cooking. Could eat at the Bolter camp just as well, but he don't fancy bachelor fare."

Target for most of the rough joking at the Garrters was "Dude" Danny Durst, a raffish youth, awkward and gangly and given to gross vanities in riding regalia. His fancy boots, studded belt, and leather cuffs were the subject of endless ribbing. He bore all with toothy grins and perused the mail order catalogues diligently in search of other startling items of apparel. He also bragged shamelessly of his ability to stick a bucking horse, a point on which he was frequently proved wrong. The many methods of inviting a horse to buck were practiced on Dude without mercy, always when he wore a favored item of gaudy garb. Scrambling up from a hard landing in a huckleberry patch, his first concern was for the pretty shirt he wore. I pitied Dude and marveled at his fortitude in pursuing his vanity, for the day of dude ranch apparel was not yet, and show-off rodeo togs were scorned by the working stockmen.

Old and young, these men of the vanishing frontier chose the same sober garb—rugged and suited to hard days in the saddle. Some of them, such as the riders I had known on Salmon River, Brick and his companions, Dace Bolter, and Pat Garrter, particularly Pat, managed to imbue the grim trappings with the splendor of romance.

The broad hat with V-rolled brim, dark trousers, shirt, vest, chaps, boots, and short leather gloves were augmented in rough weather by a heavy stag shirt and slicker or poncho. This, plus cartridge belt and its accompanying hardware, lariat, heavy saddle, and the man himself, added up to a load for even the sturdiest of saddle horses.

In consequence, unless the animal's back was treated with care, the dreaded sores developed, heralded first by a blister-like welt that, if not treated, broke out in an ever deepening and widening lesion. They were the chief misery of the pack animals and saddle horses whose backs were exposed to undue chaffing in traveling the steep terrain.

What first attracted me to Pat Garrter was his concern for the horses he rode, an attitude all too rare in this land, where men warred constantly against a harsh land. Their treatment of the animals that served them frequently matched the brutality of their surroundings. Pat's first act after unsaddling was to pass his hands slowly over the back of his horse, gently probing for the dreaded welts. If such spot were found, it was treated promptly, or if need be, the animal was put on range.

"I would rather walk than ride a sore-backed horse," he said.

Pat's father and Jim Garrter were brothers, and for many years, they'd run cattle together from adjoining river ranches. Came the day when Pat's mother, never reconciled to the isolated life of the river, had pressed hard for proper education of their three children, of whom Pat was the eldest. They'd sold out and moved to Walla Walla.

"I didn't take to it," said Pat. "The brand of this old river had burned too deep. To please the folks, I finished high school, but that was enough. Too much." He smiled engagingly. Pat had an endearing smile that transformed his serious, lean face, lighted by the fine, dark eyes of the Garrter's. He had a quality of gentleness, rare in young men of this ungentle land, and grace in movement that set him apart from the saddle-bound postures of the majority, and he managed always to be well groomed, not easy where haircuts and shaves came the hard way.

Of all the week, Saturday afternoons were the best. I was bathed and my hair washed and waved. My letters were read and their answers my only duty. The camp was deserted except for Essie and Eulie, who played school in the shade by the big room. Bess, Bib, and Young Jim were off on minor range chores, usually replenishing salt in the nearer licks. My favored spot for letter writing was the sweet, warm mat of needles under a ponderosa. All over the gentle slope of the high range, a dry breeze brought me the concert of the pines, now a low murmur, now rising in a drowsy cadence of soothing sound. Under me, a dusty drench of pine fragrance; above, a sky blue with the infinity of space.

Left to the last was Brick's letter mailed from New York. It had only passively disturbed me the previous evening, but as I reread it that afternoon, I was aware of growing rage. Now on troop transport duty, he wrote with the patronizing phrasing of a cosmopolitan informing a backwoods child of the wonders of which she might only dream. Too bad about me being "stuck in the sticks," but he would be back. He hadn't forgotten our last day together, and he'd be seeing me. He, Brick Sanson, would return! My duties in drab schools would be brightened by his account of life in a world where people lived without benefit of packhorse, bedroll, and blackened frying pan.

And return he did, for one night at a Border Days dance in Grangeville, I met him, unscathed and debonair as ever. For a few moments, we were genuinely glad to see each other, but we had made only a few rounds in our first dance when he remarked carelessly that I seemed to be "holding" my age quite well. I was, at that time, twenty. At my furious retort, we were at it again, battling with the same old zest and missed no waltz step in so doing. But it was our last dance, ever.

Fiercely I shredded Brick's letter to bits, being careful to totally destroy his service address, so that never should I be tempted to answer it. As an added precaution, I dug a hole in the pine needles and, with the heel of my boot, pounded in the scraps with vindictive jabs.

"Makes me sorry I every learned to write," drawled a pleasant masculine voice close by.

In confusion, I turned to find Pat Garrter observing me soberly from his six-foot perspective. "But you would never write a letter like that. You're not that sort of person."

He smiled and heel-squatted beside me. "Just happened along on my way up to the Eagle Rock range and saw you out here." He paused, and his gaze held mine, telling me plainly that he hadn't "happened along" at all and didn't expect me to believe his words, only his eyes.

"Yes," I said smiling happily, my mood shifting.

"Thought you might like to ride down to the Meadows Creek ranch with me tomorrow. That's our old home place. We'd have to start real early, about four o'clock to make it back by dark."

"I'd like to, very much," I said.

"That buckskin cayuse is pretty slow," he observed. "You can ride Lucky if you like."

"Oh," I said, delighted, "could I?"

I observed Lucky dozing in the background. He was a handsome Appaloosa, predominantly black with a white rump sprinkled with black patches about the size of a dollar. The country of the Salmon and Snake is notable for its fine horses, and none are more highly prized than the Appaloosa, beloved by the Nez Perce and bred by them in vast numbers during the days of the tribe's dominance.

Pat said of course I could ride Lucky, and the way he said it made me discount Brick's constant pecking about my shortcomings as a horsewoman. If I were to be trusted on the high-spirited Lucky, I must be all right. Pretty good, in fact.

Pat was looking off across the canyon.

"You know, Girl," he said softly, "I never did think I could get real loco about a schoolteacher, especially one from the city, but now—damned if I'm not beginning to see how all wrong I was."

Pleased and flattered by this disclosure, I hastened to explain that I hadn't lived long in Boise. "I grew up on this river, just like you, Pat." I said. "Only it's a different sort of river in southern Idaho through the flat sagebrush country—not wild and violent like it is here. But just the same, life wasn't easy there."

"Yes," he said quietly. "I figured you hadn't been fenced in all your life—the way you kinda fit in here."

He stood with lifted face, measuring the sun's position with the long practice of one to whom sun time is good enough. "Got to be getting along. See you this evening." He swung up on Lucky with no more apparent effort than it took to accord me a brief parting salute.

I sat there for a long time thinking of Pat: the way he rode, the way he smiled, the way he spoke, and the way he swore— just conversationally and not violently like Brick and the mule skinners who had freighted through the sagebrush country.

The Meadows Creek trip was arduous. Nearly the whole day was consumed on the trail, but with a splendid horse to ride and an attractive young man accompanying me, the excursion had its points. We were unhampered by packhorses, which gave the ride a pleasingly novel slant. It was the only journey I made that summer without the nagging worry of pack animals.

21

The Sagebrush Years

My sudden eagerness to identify myself with the hard life of those of the southern Idaho sagebrush plain had not previously been noted. Indeed, I'd carefully refrained from mentioning those dreary years to my urban friends or to Brick, whom I preferred to impress as a person of wide worldly experience. For Pat, who had freely chosen isolation in preference to the pursuit of polish, I presented a very different background and one not quite in accordance with the facts. I had known the sagebrush country only in early childhood, but I remembered enough of its hard ways to qualify with some degree of belonging in the canyon country.

The Snake was indeed the river of my tender years, and its sweeping course across southern Idaho drew to it the clans of the sagebrush plain of which my family was one. Its flow marked the pulse of a wide and desolate land, fierce with summer heat and, in winter, ravaged by wind, snow, and subzero temperatures.

We were hardy people and had to be to withstand the active hostility of this land. Its vast irrigation projects and ultimate fruitful yield were still only ideas in the minds of men who dreamed of harnessing the flow of the Snake, great, somber, and steady in its dignified course across two hundred miles of monotonous wilderness.

My mother hated this rude environment, dwelling at length on the days of her youth in the gentler surroundings of her native Kentucky. Particularly lamentable was the water scarcity; after our cistern went dry in late spring, water had to be hauled by team in great barrels from the Snake River. Not a drop could be wasted. The water wagon made the trip once a week, and often we got quite thirsty on the last day. Chickens were given the boiled vegetable water. Bathwater was used to scrub floors, dishwater went to the young cottonwoods in the yard, and none must be spilled. One was even careful to spit where it would do some good.

Fresh milk was unknown to us as children. We had a herd of wild range cattle but no milk cow, only cases of canned milk laid in each fall for the entire year. My mother used to wage frequent spirited campaigns for a "milker," but nothing ever came of it, for during the discussion of who was to extract the desired fluid, the whole idea shattered. She knew full well that her menfolk and those working periodically about the place would rather be caught running a brand than milking a cow. In that area and at that time, milking was a chore calculated to strip manhood of all dignity. Since the thought of my mother handling stock in any manner whatsoever was fantastic, we grew robustly, totally bereft of the virtues of fresh milk.

Spring was a season of anticipation, marking the release of winter's fierce grip. Then also the great bands of sheep moved across the desert to high summer range, leaving behind orphan lambs. Sprig was my first charge, presented to me by a herder as I stood at our gate watching the moving band. Almost unable to comprehend my great good fortune, I raced to the house with my precious bundle.

None of the other family members shared my joy. All regarded Sprig with the cold hostility of cattle folk. On my knees beside the weakened lamb, I pleaded with all the fervor of my six years, making rash and extravagant promises and hugging the woolly orphan to my chest. Reluctant permission was finally obtained. I was allowed to keep Sprig, and he had the best of everything I was able to obtain by fair means or foul. He followed me everywhere, and I loved him with an intensity that is still painful to remember.

Summer passed, and Sprig waxed stout and became increasingly saucy. Frequently he butted me down and tore my frocks. I still loved him with blind devotion and hoped for signs of reformation. None were evident, and his arrogance increased. Then came the bands returning from the high country to winter range. Again, watching them, my fingers tightly clutching Sprig's wool, I noted with pride that he was stouter and handsomer than other youngsters of his crop.

Without warning, he suddenly tore away from me and, in a flash, was lost to sight among his woolly brethren. I ran along the fence calling frantically, but I never saw him again. His identity was lost to me among that sea of moving backs. Blindly I ran on, sobbing and calling, on past our section line fence and out on the open range. The Basque herders and their busy dogs paid me no heed, but at last a mounted camp tender stopped my flight and listened to my hysterical explanation. Swinging me up on his saddle, he returned me home, sadly bedraggled, my face a muddy smear of dust and tears. He explained that Sprig was lost in the band, but that a good lamb had its value, and he placed a silver dollar in my hand. The cold metal gave me no comfort, but it was regarded alertly by my twelve-year-old brother, who envisioned more profitable transactions in the future.

The next spring, he rustled me quite a troop of orphans, and I tended them all summer, but I never again loved any lamb as I had the graceless Sprig. When fall came, I parted with my charges quite cheerfully and even assumed a strutting partnership with my brother in the bargaining conclaves with various sheep men.

After that, we had spending money each fall but no place to spend it, so it was pooled and went for a saddle for my brother's horse, Broomtail. I was given to understand that I would profit handsomely by the purchase of the saddle, but I was gravely doubtful when I was accorded a seat behind on the saddle skirts. Here I jogged along, saddle strings tightly wound about my hands for anchorage, while my brother carried our school lunch and attended to the manly art of horsemanship. Off across the sagebrush to the one-room school where we received our initial learning, Broomtail picked his way, avoiding gopher holes. In winter, it was a weary trek, those five miles. And on days when blizzards swept the plains, we did not go at all but studied at home under my mother's guidance. Her desire for our education was very real, so real that it was the basic cause of our moving to Boise when I was ten.

In the meantime, she did what she could, and it was by no means insignificant. The nucleus of our small library was a complete set of Dickens, from which our mother read aloud to us every night. There was no other diversion. Only rarely we had overnight guests, miners from the Buffalo Hump or Thunder Mountain whose long discussions we listened to with interest. But usually we grouped about the kitchen table in the circle of light cast by the potbellied kerosene lamp, chins cupped in palms and elbows on table, following raptly the fortunes of Little Nell, Oliver Twist, and the entire procession of Dickensian characters. They were very real to us, the people of Dickens, and the pleasant cadence of our mother's voice made up for much we did not understand in the long, tedious narratives. But all were read to us, some of them twice over, and we took with us from the sagebrush ranch a knowledge of Dickens that stood us well in high school when reports of required reading were made. Dickens, on all the lists, was widely shunned by other students in favor of brighter narratives. Not by me, however, for his plots and character sketches I could set down with no preparation, and to the progressive amazement of my teachers, I chose his titles until the entire Dickens list was exhausted, and I was forced to buckle down to initial reading.

The early autumn haze lay softly on the flat sage wastes, prefacing harsh days to come, but late summer had its excitements, for then began the hauls of the freight wagon trains. Supplies for an entire year went in this manner into the Sawtooth and Salmon River mining camps, to the home ranches of the plains. It was my pleasure to watch them pass our place, leaning over the gate and delighting in the musical ring of the hame bells on the lead teams—shrinking with pity from the crack of the long blacksnake the drivers played expertly over the backs of the laboring beasts, accompanied by vociferous profanity.

Later in the season, one of the freighters stopped at our home to unload piles of stock salt, hundred-pound sacks of flour and sugar, oatmeal, rice, beans, corn meal, dried prunes, and apples; blocks of thin, sulfurous Chinese matches; cases of lard and condensed milk; and a huge store of kerosene in five-gallon cans.

Few supplies came tinned or in glass jars, and what did were twice treasured. The empty lard buckets and kerosene cans were used until they disintegrated. Fabric of the bags, usually of coarse muslin, made dust cloths, dishtowels, curtains, and sometimes underwear. I recall a certain brand of flour, Purity, printed in green letters across the sack, which no amount of washing would efface. Unhappily for me, my mother chose to make my little panties from those sacks, the trademark remaining steadfast until their seats wore thin. My humiliation was deepened by the glee of my brother, who scoffed and dubbed me "Purity-Pants." Wrapping paper, string, and the few paper bags that came our way were all useful. All were treasured and used again and again. Trash disposal was a minor chore to be undertaken only during spring and fall house cleaning. There was never much to be thrown away.

The first Christmas tree of my memory was a five-foot sagebrush, for evergreen trees were quite beyond the hopes of a family at our distance from either commercial or native supply. My brother searched for the tallest sagebrush in the area, tying his rope to it and snaking it home behind Broomtail. My mother dipped its branches in a green dye solution, but the gray sage assumed even a drearier shade, so she stripped it and wrapped the trunk and branches with strips of white muslin.

It was to my entranced gaze a wondrous sight, festooned with strings of popcorn and adorned with candles, dainty twisted tapers set in tin holders that clamped on the branches. At its top was poised a cardboard angel outlined in festive tinsel, a splendid creature that occupied a place of honor among my treasures and enhanced many a Christmas tree thereafter. Up through the years I have beheld many of America's most lavish yule displays, but none has dimmed the splendor of that, my sagebrush Christmas tree.

After those harsh years, we received the benefits of suburbia with gratitude. Our initial wonder at the luxury of electricity and of water that ran effortlessly from a faucet soon subsided. All that and more, we believed, were necessities. Disenchantment was a rude shock, but it is fortunate that I came to the land of the great canyons with a background of privation.

My spirit was considerably toughened by those ten years in the sagebrush.

22

Forever Packhorse

Saddle horse and pack train is still the only method of transporting humanity and its possessions through the backcountry of the Salmon, Snake, and Clearwater. So far, humankind has devised no other means of moving their goods off this land's arteries of travel, and there is nothing to indicate that beasts of burden will soon be supplanted.

The art of packing requires special skill and knowledge, and expert packers are always in demand. A novice can run into trouble aplenty and do untold damage to a pack string in even one trip. Saddling requires know-how, for pack saddles are double cinched, and if the rear cinch be drawn too tight, it binds the animal's belly, causing him to buck, damaging and scattering equipment. There are fine points to lashing a pack. Most difficult to throw is the diamond hitch. The Lang hitch is popular in some sections and for some purposes, and the squaw hitch is generally used by the uninitiated.

Every ranch has its blacksmith shop, every camp its improvised smithy and equipment. Every stockman who really works at it, every hired man, must know the art of shoeing horses. Constant vigilance for the feet of mounts and pack animals is vital, for the terrain multiplies foot hazards many times over. Iron grinding against rock quickly wears thin. Frequently, shoes are "thrown" in the fulcrums of rock crevices. Few days pass during the packing season when there are not shoeing chores to be done.

In a well-managed pack train under the supervision of a skillful packer there is beauty, rhythm, and grace. A packer who knows his business can look back over his string and spot instantly a slipping or unbalanced pack, for it is marked by an animal out of rhythm, a creature in pain fighting its load. Balance is imperative, for an unbalanced pack will soon rub and chafe a horse's back and cause the frightful sores so prevalent in a country where steep going invites the shifting of a load.

Only a few of the elite, the highly prized riding horses and saddle mules, escaped the scars of packing. Most are marked by small, white patches of hair on backs, which grow over old scar tissue, and there are permanent bare stripes across haunches and breast, caused by rubbing of the breeching and breast straps.

The old sawbuck pack saddle was the first type devised and is still widely used. The sawbuck forks hold the straps of the baglike alforjas, which swing from each side. Usually they are made of canvas or leather. The packing boxes fit into the alforjas. The sawbuck forks, centered from four to six inches above the animal's back, cause undue strain and allow the pack to swing and shift with movement up and down trails.

Early in the century, a saddle intended to ease the lot of pack animals was devised by Glenn Robinett of Kooskia on the Clearwater. He carved the two sides of the wooden saddletree to fit the back of a specific horse. They were fastened together by a crescent-shaped iron strap, smithied to a correct fit, its loop providing a focal point for securing lash ropes. If the saddle were later to be used for another animal, Robinett urged that he be allowed to correct the fit, giving careful attention to changes in the tree, shaping, and reworking of the iron strap. Robinett, a humane man who had regarded the suffering of pack animals for years with great distaste, produced "tailored-to-fit" pack saddles and took great pride in so doing. He called his design the "half-breed," since it partook of the best qualities of the sawbuck and the Mexican aparejo.

Later, the Decker brothers, Johnny and Bert, developed the half-breed commercially, and the Decker saddle came to be widely used in the Idaho packing country. Its success was acknowledged by the forest service, and through that medium, it spread to all sections of the West. The Deckers were famed for their skill as packers, keeping more than one hundred packhorses and mules at their headquarters on the Clearwater. On one occasion, they packed a complete logging operation into the St. Maries country, a feat which was generally deemed impossible. So skillful were they in balancing packs that they frequently packed without lashing.

As the second half of the century dawned, short landing strips augmented the highway and boat routes, but where the road station received passengers and freight, where the boat edged up to its lonely bar landing, where the light plane came to rest on the scant strip, there waited, and still waits, the pack train to begin the task of moving commodities over trails that tax the nimbleness of a mountain goat.

23

"EE-DA-HOW"

Down past the school camp corral and over a sloping flat of "cheat," a grass that relentlessly nudged out scattered stands of bunch grass, was a faint trail to the edge of the canyon's highest rim. Here spread an awesome panorama and the best view of the great canyon that I was ever to obtain.

Every morning of that summer, I awoke early, for we retired at darkness. Reading or writing by the light of a lantern at the cook tent table drew hordes of mosquitoes. We frequently built smudges outside the door of each sleeping tent and later tied the flaps tight, thus eliminating most of the wretched pests, but to the light they swarmed in hungry conquest. Accordingly, I went to bed as the late northern twilight deepened into night and lay quietly in the mornings, mindful not to disturb the two sleeping girls. After I discovered the vantage point on the rim, it became my habit to rise; dress with caution; and, accompanied by Maxie, walk out in the sweet, cool dawn to watch the sun rise over the Seven Devils.

Up to this time, I recall no special preference for solitude, indeed quite the contrary. But during these school camp days, its achievement became an active obsession, projected by the fact that to be alone even for a few minutes was almost impossible. Every hour of these days and nights was shared with the children. They were ever with me. I frequently brooded over the fact that, though isolated in one of the continent's most desolate and thinly populated regions, I was beset with companionship that I was under contract to share. To be left alone, deserted, in this ragged frontier would have been terrifying. I didn't want to be left alone, but I did, for reasons unanalyzed, want to be able to choose occasional solitude.

This secret daily hour on the rim, therefore, approached communion. It was my own—a chording of the faint spark within humanity with the deep spirit of the natural world. Being myself little more than a child, I did not identify these groping's toward maturity. I only knew that this interlude of renewal prepared me in some subtle manner for the day ahead—gave me a respite of at least one hour away from my charges.

The daily excursion had advantages other than the esthetic. Passing the corral where our horses were confined nights, I always paused to see if our sore-backed horses were improving under the ministrations of Young Jim and Clem, who were charged with bathing their backs each evening with alum water. Always we had sore-backed horses at the school camp, for as bad cases developed under the merciless packing regime necessary to keep the summer camps supplied, they were relegated to the school string for rest, the only sure cure. The membership of our remuda, therefore, was fluid, Riley and Old Mouse being the only ones with us all summer.

Much controversy over the word Idaho has stirred up a

story that it was originally a contraction of the Shoshoni word "ee-da-how," which, translated, is an exclamation of joy at the sun coming down the mountain and signified that there was, to the Native American mind, something very pleasant in this first breaking of light over the high places. After witnessing the fingers of day stealing with ever-changing shades of lavender, mauve, and deep purple down the majestic sides of Old Monument, He-Devil peak, and the lesser Devils, I can well understand the reverence with which primitive mind greeted the coming down of the light.

First, pale chartreuse rimmed the jagged horizon, changing swiftly as translucent opal broke through the smooth skin of night. Exquisite shades lay in lagoons along the stony summits of the canyon's east battlement, which finally stood against a sapphire sky, the deep clefts refilling with rosy pools of enchantment.

Rim by rim, the harmony of color deepened to dusky purple in the pit of the chasm, which even in midday lay in shadow. Six thousand feet below me flowed the Snake with fury and volume, but from my lofty view, it seemed only a green thread. Its rapids, mighty as breakers, were mere flecks of white.

The Seven Devils, forever rigid on the horizon, broke along their lower reaches into forest slopes, unfolding in endless succession, their ridges furred in a mantle of somber green. They ran long, linking into each other, and as early sun strafed them with shafts of splendor, breeze chorded daybreak, and a faint sigh wafted across the canyon.

When I was seated on the rim of the vast abyss, the beauty

of these dawns sustained, recreated my spirit. Maxie, leaning lightly away from his crippled forefoot, pressed against me and gazed solemnly across the void. Two small specks of life, we crouched together on the edge of the continent's deepest declivity, and through our precious senses, something of its grandeur and magnitude flowed through our hearts.

24

Old Sugar

We were occupied in the daily dictionary class that July afternoon when the barking of Jupe far down in the draw apprised us that something unusual moved along the Rim Trail. Jupe was the MacDeen dog, a large bobtail border collie, and he stayed always with the horses, sleeping at the corral at night and ranging about them out on the rims during the day. His deep bay was urgent. It hit hysterical tones, drawing steadily nearer and indicating that he was traveling with considerable speed to a confluence at the Rim Trail. Tiny, aroused from her afternoon nap at the door of the cook tent, made it a duet, and Maxie rushed from under my desk to a stance outside the schoolhouse, growling angrily and gazing southward. Classes came to a pause, and we crowded to the door.

"It's old Sugar," announced Clem. "I can tell by the way Jupe barks. And he's got those pesky goats along. We'll have to get the dogs tied, for they sure hate them goats."

Clem and Young Jim departed immediately in an attempt to intercept Jupe, and Bib started for Tiny, but the dogs seemed possessed. Maxie, usually so tractable, danced away from me. Tiny, likewise elusive, tore about in a frenzy of rage.

Maryadee pawed at me urgently. "I'd better go hide the sugar," she said. "Else we won't have any." She widened her eyes at me knowingly.

Having been told of Old Sugar and his amazing affinity for sweets, together with his cunning methods of acquiring any that he might chance to see, I bade her go at once, while we resumed our efforts to catch the dogs. Jupe sounded close and was, I concluded, as yet unfettered when our visitor appeared, a heavy, shambling figure clad in baggy corduroys and several shirts held together with an ingenious arrangement of odd buttons and safety pins. From under a brimless felt hat, long, grizzled hair fell to his shoulders. But his features were obscured by an amazing crop of whiskers. He carried a pack and a stout walking stick and was flanked by a pair of stalwart tan and white goats.

We abandoned our attempts to catch the dogs to gaze at the peculiar trio, and at this moment Jupe, encouraged by the proximity of reinforcement, made his appearance. With a burst of barking, he dived at the rearmost goat. Instantly, the camp was a bedlam. All three dogs entered the fray. The goats stamped their feet and made butting runs at their antagonists, while Old Sugar laid about with the stick. We were all in it by that time, and the dust of battle eddied up about us. I drew the young children back out of range of the swinging stick, hoping that the three boys could cope with the dogs. The goats, in a fury, charged left and right and their master's stick swung lustily. The din and dust were incredible.

Clem at last had Jupe. He and Young Jim dragged him struggling toward the corral. Bib followed with Tiny, and Essie ran to the packsaddles to get rope for Maxie, who was being held by the two little boys. The dust began to settle, and amenities were in order.

"I'm sorry, er ...Mr. Sugar." I cast about hopelessly for the man's real name. "We tried to get the dogs tied before you came." Judging from the yelps of pain occasioned as Sugar laid about with the stick, I knew full well that any casualties were on our side, but the social proprieties prompted me to add, "I hope the goats aren't hurt."

The goats were definitely not hurt. They stood and stared at us with pale, unwinking eyes, occasionally stamping their feet and lowering their heads warningly.

"Hex and Het'll hold their own with any dogs," returned the old man with fine scorn. "We come to visit the school," he added.

"Why, yes," I agreed lamely. "Won't you come in."

But Sugar was already headed for the school, and so were the goats.

The boys, having tied the three dogs at the corral, returned, and an attempt was made to resume our class. Seating himself on a bench at the rear of the room, Sugar removed his packsack, depositing it beside him. The goats stood immobile just outside the door, gazing intently at the corral where the barking continued. Occasionally, they stamped their feet or uttered insulting bleats, which caused the din to arise with new vigor.

Sugar gazed at me with colorless eyes, like pebbles in a filmed pool, rimmed by lower lids that sagged away revealing crescents of red membrane. Finally, he opened his untidy shirts, displaying a chesty expanse of shaggy, gray hair, and began to scratch himself vigorously. A stout goaty odor permeated the room, increasing when Hex and Het, bored with teasing the dogs, wandered in and began an investigation of the room's appointments.

I arose resolutely. This, I felt, was not to be tolerated.

"Really, Mr. Sugar—" I began but was stopped by a violent movement from Young Jim, who gazed at me warningly, active apprehension in his dark eyes. I hesitated and then motioned to him, and he followed me down to the cook tent.

"Crazy or not, we can't put up with those goats in the schoolroom," I announced flatly.

"Pa says to humor him and not ever get him mad," the lad argued earnestly. "He'll only come once. If he don't get sugar, he never comes around again till the next term. He's kinda sore already—about the dogs, I mean. I can tell by the way he just sits and don't say anything. We've got to make out with him the best we can."

Somberly, we returned to the schoolhouse.

During our absence, Hex had found the chalk box, tipped it over, and was mouthing our precious supply of chalk. I made an attempt to retrieve it, but he stamped his hooves so fiercely that I retreated in haste to my desk. Het was at our blackboard, a scant strip of painted canvas tacked to the wall. She had found a frayed edge and was working at it, making ripping sounds as the rotten fabric tore away. One corner was already shredded.

The children gazed in fascination at the destruction, for this pathetic blackboard was the room's chief attraction, and writing on it was a coveted privilege for every child in the school. To sit thus and watch its demolition, together with the wanton waste of our short supply of chalk was too much to be endured. Essie's eyes were on me in pleading supplication. Her stiff pigtails trembled with agitation.

Sugar, making no attempt to discipline his wretched charges, continued to stare at me, occasionally emitting strange clucking sounds, blowing out his cheeks and allowing the air to escape through his lips with a bubbling sound. The atmosphere grew goatier by the minute; the chalk crunching and canvas ripping continued, and our guest stared on, blubbering noisily.

I arose with resolution, avoiding the eyes of Young Jim.

"School is dismissed," I proclaimed loudly. "We'll begin chores at once."

Books were laid aside, and a hurried exodus began.

"Hex! Het!" roared Sugar, picking up his packsack and stick.

Instantly, the vandalism ceased and the two creatures bolted for the door.

"That does it," I muttered with satisfaction, following the procession out, locking the door, and slipping the key to Bib, who always began his cleaning as soon as school closed. "We'll take up school again as soon as he leaves," I whispered.

My hopes of ridding ourselves of the goaty trio were quite futile, I soon realized, for Sugar lumbered after us down to the cook tent, enthroned himself on the heap of pack saddles outside, and gazed with interest through the open tent flaps at our preparations for supper. The goats stood by, staring at us with sinister, pale eyes. The barking at the corral began with renewed vigor.

Our menu that night was beef boiled with potatoes, the usual thick gravy, fresh string beans and red raspberries, the latter two items having been packed up from the river gardens. The berries were reduced to jam through the process but were eaten with relish nonetheless. In shortcake manner, the mess was spread over light bread and topped with sugar and condensed milk.

Young Jim and Clem rounded up the horses, taking Old Mouse, matriarch of the remuda, who was confined days in the corral for her influence in keeping the band close to camp. I saw them riding her double out toward the rims, and presently their familiar yipping "Hi-yi" came from down in the timber of the next gully. Soon they hove into sight, driving the horses up the draw, Young Jim on Old Mouse and Clem riding his own saddle horse with an improvised rope hackamore. In a cloud of dust, they swept past the camp and up to the water trough. I hurried up to intercept them there.

"Is he going to stay for supper?" I inquired ominously.

"It's the quickest way of making him believe there is no sugar here," replied Clem.

Back at the cook tent, Maryadee had a fire going in the camp stove, and the pot of meat, whose cooking had been started at the breakfast hour, was emitting steam. Essie was setting the table, and I noted with resignation that places were laid for nine. Maryadee sidled close to me as I pared the potatoes at the packing case we used for a worktable.

"When we get ready to have the shortcake," she whispered, "we'll all feel bad, cause there's no sugar. You, too." She rounded her eyes at me significantly.

"Where is it—the sugar?"

"Under our bunk, all covered up with quilts."

Sugar still roosted on his perch watching our every move. The goats had settled down beside him, and for a merciful period, the racket at the corral had ceased. The old fellow's mustache, long and flowing, worked up and down eagerly as he observed our supper preparations. He unfastened his series of shirts and again began the scratching operation.

"He's got lice," whispered Maryadee fiercely. "Great, big

old gray backs, Ma says. 'Cause once Pa had to stay at his shack all night, and when he got home, Ma made him skin off all his clothes and scrub, while she boiled every stick he had on. Pa said it was awful in that shack 'cause the goats slept there too," she concluded with satisfaction.

I heard the horses being driven to the corral for the night, and a fine screen of dust floated in the tent. The two little boys, carrying wood to replenish the rick outside the tent, were engaged in their usual argument as to who had carried the most loads. Sounds from the school indicated that Bib was at his janitorial duties. Everything was in the usual norm except the dreadful, hairy old man who sat silently watching us, flanked by his noxious pets. I felt suddenly apprehensive and wished Young Jim and Clem would hurry back.

At last the meal was on the table. We were assembled, and Sugar was motioned to my usual place at the head of the table. The eight of us crowded on the two benches, the movement being definitely away from our uncouth guest. He at once began looking eagerly about, peering into cups and serving dishes. I watched him, fascinated, fearing he would snatch the children's food from their plates, but it soon became evident that he had little interest for anything visible on our board.

Graniteware cups were placed at each plate filled with diluted milk, and when Sugar drank, he held the cup in both hands and gulped noisily. He emerged with a good share of the liquid clinging to his mustache, but this he dispatched by sucking the hirsute adornment into his mouth and vacuuming it vigorously. At this demonstration, I lost all interest in food. But the children, in no way affected, attacked the fare with energy. And in due time, the servings of shortcake were before us, sans sugar.

Again, Sugar searched the table expectantly and turned to peer in and around our supply cupboard. The children made no move to partake of the dessert.

"No sugar?" rumbled the old man, fixing us with a fierce stare.

"No sugar," Young Jim responded quickly.

And immediately all the youngsters took up the chorus. "No sugar!" they chanted. "No sugar! No sugar!" There was a violent shaking of heads all around.

At this, our guest looked downcast. He dropped his head and gazed fixedly at the table muttering, "No sugar."

And again, the children chimed in like actors taking a cue. I too, played my part, looking properly sorrowful and shaking my head sadly.

Suddenly Sugar raised his head, and his poor, red-rimmed eyes looked almost intelligent. He arose and went out to his packsack, extracted a tin can, and returned. Removing the lid, he passed it to me. It was nearly full of sugar, definitely gray in color, as it had been sifted many times through his grimy paws in the manner of a miser fondling gold. Repelled, I drew back. Every eye was upon me. Sugar leaned near, breathing noisily and staring at me frighteningly. Young Jim, sitting next to me, nudged me with urgency. I dipped in and sprinkled the grimy substance over my shortcake, reflecting doggedly that, come what might, nothing could induce me to eat it. The can went the rounds, the youngsters helping themselves without inhibition. What was left Sugar dumped on his shortcake, spooning it up to the last grain.

After eating his fill, he walked to the door, shouldered his pack, and left without a word, followed by Hex and Het.

I sat wearily amid the bedlam of comment that followed his departure.

"Maybe we should have replaced his sugar," I suggested.

"Aw, he's got plenty," scoffed Bib. "Has it cached all around his place, and the packers are always bringing him more. Pa says he's probably got hundreds of pounds of sugar buried in tin cans. Why, if we once gave him sugar, he'd be here every day."

"You're sure he won't come back?" I inquired anxiously.

I was assured vehemently that he would not—until next year at least.

Old Sugar paid us the only classroom visit of the term, and it had completely disrupted our afternoon. Most of the chores were done, but the sun was still four hours from setting. I thought of a resumption of classes but had not the heart to order this anticlimax. There was never time for play at the school camp; our schedule was rigid, and it was amazing how much time was consumed in the mechanics of living.

I thought of the deep pools along Race Creek. Here trout

abounded, for scant fishing was done by the folk of the summer camps, and sportsmen were unknown in that rugged hinterland. Race Creek, like the other numerous feeders to the Snake, was virgin fishing. The children would be hungry again before bedtime, our usual supper having been consumed hours ahead of time; I, too, for my meal had been completely spoiled. We could catch a mess of trout before sundown, be back at camp, and have them fried before dark.

"Untie the dogs, and we'll feed them," I announced. "Let's get on with the dishes, girls, while Clem and Jim get the horses saddled. And, Bib, get your fish lines, and see if you can rustle some bait."

25

The Big Brass

Travelers along the Rim Trail averaged two or three a day, usually lone horsemen and occasional pack outfits, the long mule trains of the forestry service being the most frequently seen. Passing by our door, brief amenities were usually exchanged. The olive-green garb and stiff-brimmed felts distinguished the men of the forest service, whose role in the early days of their department's jurisdiction was far from a happy one. Preaching the doctrine of conservation to a people reared to exploit resources resulted in open hostility and, often, vindictive behavior by those whose cooperation with a planned economy was sought.

The native rancher, accustomed to unrestricted use of public grazing, accepted with ill grace the allotting of privileges on the national forest reserve. The written applications, together with oral questions put by the resident ranger, were fiercely resented, for these people were reticent about their personal affairs, their possessions, and their past activities and future plans. Those who asked such questions were unpopular, but the ranger had no choice.

Methods of overgrazing had already destroyed wide areas of the nutritious bunch grass, which was replaced with stands of ragged cheat, worthless as forage. Allowing more cattle or sheep in a given area than the grass could support with any hope of survival was sternly dealt with by the forestry men. It was obvious that the stockmen's estimate of how many head an area would support was much higher than the ranger's figure. That argument continues to this day (1970s).

Regular salting at accustomed spots was advocated as a means of keeping stock within their given range. The salvage of springs through simple protective measures, the killing of game only in season—all were rules difficult to enforce, for care of the native forage and wildlife came hard to a people accustomed to employing savage measures against a savage land.

The rangers frequently found it easier to deal with the big cattle or sheepmen. To them, use of the high summer range was vital. They were, therefore, more amenable to pressures and could be forced to comply with regulations through threat that grazing permits would not be renewed. The scores of small-fry stockmen and homesteaders whose negligible herds could "get by" multiplied the ranger's problems many times over. Acting on the privilege of taking two hundred dollars' worth of timber from the reserve for buildings or improvements, they frequently cut the trees and left them where they fell, thus scarring their ranger's district and bringing down upon him the wrath of his supervisor for allowing fire hazards to exist.

The killing of deer out of season was also a practice that led to endless altercation, as was the manufacture of various vitriolic messes of moonshine, which came mainly from the homesteaders and found eager purchasers throughout the canyon country. Although the rangers stoutly denied their interest or jurisdiction in the concoction of these unlawful brews, they were nonetheless blamed for informing the law when a raid was made. This occurrence was so infrequent that it set the whole country agog, for few revenue men possessed the temerity to invade the canyon country, and those who did nearly always found themselves "jobbed." News of their coming was relayed ahead in sufficient time for the embryo distiller to conceal evidence of his activity.

Some of the men reared in the country found places in the forest service as rangers and packers, and they were tolerated for their understanding of ways and conditions. But the "schooled" ranger or supervisor trained by precept for his job had a rough time of it. He was simply unacceptable, for the natives particularly resented those whom they figured had "learned it in books" and were constantly alerted to catch them in the promotion of impractical ideas.

Such a man was Anthony Stettin, who scaled to greater heights in authority then any department representative who had ever invaded the canyon districts. His spot visitations throughout the West that summer were designed to obtain firsthand knowledge for the edification of the department, and he was out to glean his knowledge the hard way. Unheralded he came, clothed in the regal authority of the federal government, correctly uniformed, and sitting his saddle with the stiff misery of the uninitiated. The first time he passed our camp with Jack Downey, the resident ranger, he accorded us little more than a brief nod accompanied by an incredulous stare at our scarecrow camp and ragged equipment. Ranger Downey paused, as was his habit, for an agreeable word, but his companion rode straight ahead with no backward glance.

"A government big-bug," Downey confided. There was awe in his voice and pride in his bearing.

I watched with pleasurable interest as Downy rode in the company of so great a person. Not so the children. Their hostile stares followed the pair as they disappeared around the turn.

"A high mucky-muck, I betcha," commented Young Jim.

"Gar, did you see the polish on his boots?" exclaimed Clem.

"Tony-Toes," shouted Bib. "That's what he is. Old Tony-Toes!"

"Those smart-aleck forestry men," observed Maryadee with venom. "Always snooping around. And two years back, one of them took our teacher and never brought her back, that's what!"

"Maryadee," I said severely, "no one forced her to go. She went willingly. And we'll talk no more of it."

I had heard the teacher-napping tale with embellishments from Mrs. Mac during my first weekend in the MacDeen's camp; the story was intended certainly to impress me with the horrible example set by a predecessor.

"He was a reckless young rake who packed that summer for the forest service," Mrs. Mac had said. "Somehow him and this teacher managed to see a good bit of each other right from the start. She'd been here hardly a month mind you, when he came along one morning packing back to Homestead. Had an extra saddle horse. Took her and her things, and off they rode. Never saw hide ner hair of either one again, for you can be sure that caper finished him with the forest service. And that teacher! Left those poor children alone at the camp. A fine thing."

Knowing the ability of the "poor children" to shift for themselves, I was only passively horrified by the tale. "Must have been quite a blow to Mr. MacDeen." I envisioned with pleasure his discomfiture at the escape of one of his catches.

"Mac was fit to be tied," she stated. "Swore he'd do something about it, but he never did. Couldn't get another teacher that summer either."

"Serves him right," I said recklessly. "Getting teachers in here under false pretenses!"

Mrs. Mac fixed me with a stern eye. "No teacher has to stay here if she doesn't want to, but we do think we might be told of her intentions."

"Well, I'm staying," I said. "To the bitter end."

Returning alone the next week from the forestry office at Joseph, the "Big Brass" rode past the school camp shortly before supper. He stopped, smiled, and raised his stiff felt.

His face was lined with fatigue; the close-cropped mustache looked a little ragged, and he could have done with a haircut. The formerly polished boots were sadly scuffed, and dust lay heavy upon them.

"I didn't realize when I passed last week with Downey that this was a school. It has none of the ordinary signs. Most unusual. I want to commend you on carrying out such an assignment. I shall mention it in my department reports."

"Yes," I said, striving to match his impeccable diction, "the school is on forest reserve land, I believe."

"A most worthy use," he stated pedantically.

"Mr. Downey is not with you?" I felt an insatiable curiosity as to why this greenest of all greenhorns had been left unguarded on this of all hazardous trails.

"Downey has other duties than escorting me about. There is much—much to be done here," said the Big Brass. I suspected that Downey had received considerable instruction straight from the book, and I felt sorry for him. The man's lot was already hard enough.

The children gathered beside me in a tight knot. Silently they observed the Big Brass with bright, suspicious eyes.

"You're not intending to make Homestead tonight surely," I said, noting the fatigue of man and horse.

"Only to our temporary camp a little past Pan Creek."

"That's still nearly two hours from here," I remarked.

"So strange, measuring distance by hours. But after this trip, it is quite understandable." He shifted slightly in the saddle, but only his eyes mirrored the pain of movement.

"Would you have supper with us?" I inquired impulsively. "It is nearly ready for the table."

"I would with pleasure." There was no hesitancy in the acceptance.

Painfully he removed himself from the saddle.

Hostile silence and no movement from the group at my side.

"Jim," I said sharply, disconcerted at their ghoulish behavior, "will you care for the horse?"

Reluctantly Young Jim slouched forward, loosed the cinch, and led the animal up to the water trough.

It was a strange meal, the Big Brass and I carrying the total load of conversation. I tried by every effort known to me to induce these children to show some friendliness, but all ate silently, eyes on plates.

"Such well-mannered young people," the Big Brass finally remarked. "And this young lady," indicating Essie who sat at his right, "reminds me of my own little daughter in Washington. Not at all like me, understand, but a beautiful blond like her mother."

At this, Essie wriggled, and her taut braids vibrated. It was probably the first compliment ever accorded the plain child. Suddenly she flashed our guest one of her rare smiles, and something certainly akin to loveliness transformed her face. That broke the ice, and the tension around the table lessened.

After supper, we all trooped to the schoolhouse for an inspection requested by the Big Brass. In the fading daylight, the room's scant equipment, its pitiful bareness, was sharply accented. The tragedy of the blackboard was related by Essie, who stuck to the big man's side like a small, nondescript burr.

"Incredible," said the Brass.

To me, he remarked in a low tone, "I have never seen a schoolroom—any room—with so little. How do you manage?"

"We do all right," I said. "We get the job done."

He eyed me thoughtfully. "I'm sure you do, but still ..."

As Young Jim cinched his saddle, I covertly suggested that he and Clem get their horses and escort the Big Brass along his way. "At least through that mean Pan Creek Canyon," I whispered. "No telling what may happen to him alone, and it's getting dark."

"No big loss if something did happen." Young Jim's tone was cold. "Besides, his horse will get him there."

"Offer to anyway," I insisted sharply.

But the Big Brass would have none of it. He was quite

capable of taking care of himself, he said, and so he rode off, stiff and uncompromising in his saddle.

Ten days later, a forest service packer stopped and unloaded at the school a wondrous cargo.

"Orders from the boss to handle with care," he said, "and an installation job for me."

Dismantled and packed in four sections was a blackboard that would have added glamour to the walls of any city schoolroom. There were also white and colored chalk and a dozen entrancing books of history, travel, and adventure.

"We'd ought to write him a letter," said Young Jim.

26

White-Water Runners

A canvas mail sack hangs from a stake on a desolate rock-strewn bar. There are many such on either side of the Snake above Lewiston, after roads disappear and grim crags dominate the landscape. Each marks the landing for a sheep or cattle outfit, but habitation is screened from view by forbidding rock and rim. To deposit several hundred pounds of food and supplies at one of these bleak spots seems pure folly to the uninitiated boat passenger, who thinks surely it is abandonment and a total waste.

There is a faint cry seeming to come from the heavens. The boat traveler looks up. In the delirium of rock far above moves a pack train, creeping down a switchback, now disappearing from view behind gigantic outcrops, now reappearing to inch along the rock face of a precipice. The man in the lead raises his arm in the familiar wide salute. His companion at the rear of the train gives out with the traditional high-toned, "Hi-yai." Faintly it echoes back from the sheer rock walls.

The merchandise on the deserted bar is not abandoned. It is merely exchanging one mode of transit for another.

The gallant riverboat, *Idaho* powered by two Winton-six motors backs and then cuts out into the current.

Ahead looms the fury of Wild Goose Rapids.

The men who successfully ran the turbulent water of the Snake and Salmon came up the hard way. Mute evidence of the failure of those who strove to conquer without benefit of experience is still seen along those rivers' courses—part of a bow nearly covered with silt and flood debris, another vital boat section derisively flung in a cliff crevice by high water, engine parts rusting on a lonely bar.

Since the days when Lewis and Clark heeded the warning of their Indian guide, Toby, and turned back from the forbidding water of the upper Salmon to seek their way over Lolo Pass and down the Clearwater to the present site of Lewiston, men have battled ceaselessly to conquer the arrogant waters of the Salmon. A one-way conquest is the best they have been able to achieve, as of 1970.

Captain Harry Gueleke negotiated his first successful downstream passage in the 1890s when he piloted a flat-bottom scow from Salmon City, at the foot of the Bitter Root, through bludgeoning rapids to the union with the Snake and thence to Lewiston. There the vessel was ripped apart and sold as lumber while the captain returned overland to Salmon City to begin construction of a similar scow for the next trip down. It came to be an annual risk each fall during low water and soon attracted sportsmen, scientists, and thrill seekers from every part of the nation and from abroad. The trip required from two to three weeks, allowing for night camps, friendly bars, and the varied inclinations of passengers for research and side excursions.

I saw Captain Gueleke and his boat at close range only once during my years on the Salmon, and that was on an October evening when he tied up for the night at Billie Creek on the lower river. A group of us rode down from Fly Blow, the Jones's summer camp on Joseph Plains, to greet the captain and his party, talking with them for some time around their campfire on the Billie Creek bar.

He had a trio of geologists aboard that trip, who came to study the general canyon structure and particularly the nature of the Idaho Batholith, which, they informed us, was one of the world's largest granite masses. They also told us quite frankly that they were amazed at the alert and enlightened people who inhabited one of America's most impregnable sections. But this I had already learned for myself, for during the seven years I'd lived and taught in the heart of Idaho's great primitive area, I met but one illiterate person, and he was a recent arrival from the state of Tennessee.

For nearly forty years, Captain Gueleke continued to pilot his strange-looking craft down the waters of the Salmon, earning for the river the descriptive title "River of No Return," for man in contest with this most ferocious of flows must be content with the measure of conquest tolerated.

Battle-scarred veteran of the Snake's white water is the *Idaho*, still running her course after more than thirty years of service up to the head at Johnson's Bar. Captain E. G.

McFarlane, pioneer pilot of the lower Snake, made his historic run to five miles above Pittsburg Landing in 1911, using the thirty-five-foot, gasoline-powered *Flyer*. And during the century's early decades, he and Pres Brewrink, piloting the *Clipper*, made river navigation history on the Snake.

It requires experience, courage, and constant vigilance on the part of the white-water boatmen, for channel changes, particularly at the location of rapids, must be carefully studied after high water, normally in late May and early June.

The Snake, like the Salmon, is terrible in flood. Deep, swift, and treacherous at best, both are to be avoided at all cost during high water when runoff from the high country's big snows brings them to a stage of frenzy with which no sane man dares to contend. Great trees, uprooted, are flung about like splinters in the crest of the flood, which rises to frightening heights in mid channel. Occasionally, a tree will suddenly poise upright and then plunge vertically into a whirlpool, its one hundred-foot length instantly sucked down to oblivion. It may emerge several hundred yards downstream, stripped of bark and branches, starkly white in its agony, or it may never again be identified as a tree, its substance ground to shreds in the cruel granite teeth of the river channel. Boulders of unbelievable size and weight are rolled so savagely that thunder fills the canyons.

Results of this colossal pounding throw dangerous obstructions in what was, during the past season, a clear channel. To such changes, the river navigator must be constantly alerted.

During the era of my Hells Canyon sojourn, travelers on the Snake River boats were mainly stockmen and their families, miners, prospectors, and men of the forest service. The shipping of their supplies, together with contract to carry the mail, formed the basis of the boat business. As soon as high water receded in early summer, shipment of the wool crop, collected at the bar landings, was the main cargo of the riverboats. In fall, it was the transportation of year-round supplies to the river ranchers or the small and far-flung mine operations.

Passengers "out" on sweltering June days were jammed among woolsacks and flung about roughly through stretches of white water. They disembarked at the Lewiston dock looking and smelling like bags of wool, sheep-like and chastened in spirit, for in addition to paying boat fare, they pitched in and helped with loading or unloading at the various landings. It was customary and facilitated progress. The harder they labored, the sooner they would be on their way again and the final destination reached. The captain judged the speed of his trip by counting the noses of his male passengers. They all added up to that many deckhands, for they worked with the cargo or they got nowhere.

Nor did the pilots lack in appreciation for varied services rendered, for they cheerfully went about town errands for river families, taking on anything from legal business to the purchase of baby clothes. Between them and Mrs. Ruth Sapp, proprietor of the Lewiston store, which traditionally filled merchandise orders for most of the people of the canyon country, they got the job done. All such items went on the client's account at Sapp's store to be settled at the end of the season. Frequently, gold dust was the medium of payment.

But River passage "in" and "out" had its points for wayfarers, providing a medium of news exchange for the river people. Newcomers were greeted; new friends were made, and old acquaintances renewed. Episodes of the range were recounted. Rumors of new mining activities were appraised. Gossip and bits of personal scandal were savored. It was the best possible medium for discovering what went on along the river, in its far-flung ranges, and in mining country.

Today (the 1970s) new captains and new boats are on the river. Their missions vary from carrying the mail to deluxe trips for vacationing sightseers. There are facilities for those who seek to hook the giant sturgeon and for hunters too, in season. And still is there the traditional line for ranch supplies and the annual wool hauls, though the stops have now dwindled in number since big ownership moved in to consolidate holdings.

Amid the new luxury craft, the old *Idaho*, dean of white-water runners, is not without honor. Scarred and punished throughout the years but still strong of heart, she runs the lower Snake, taking on cargos to the capacity of her eight-ton rating and discharging her duties with the old spirit, when she was queen of the river.

27

Zero Week

Fortunately, I was well established in the routine of the school camp before that week in mid-August. Had the near tragic events of those five days occurred during the first faltering weeks of my stay, it is likely that I would have sought any means to terminate my contract and get myself out of the country. Most of what happened we blamed on the weather.

It was one of the infrequent weekends I spent at the MacDeen camp, and I was in no happy mood when we left early Monday morning, having, I felt, been unduly put upon. Mrs. Mac had worried endlessly at my preference for the Garrter camp and its attractive male personnel. Her plaintive repetition, "But I'm sure you're always welcome here, and we do our best to make you comfortable," only added to my fury. I was irked. I vowed it should be my last stay with the MacDeens as our little procession took to the trail. The dawn hours were already oppressive with the only extreme heat we were to know that summer.

At the forks of the trail we waited for the Garrter's and finally rode on without them. They arrived late at school,

Young Jim explaining that their pack had slipped and that he had to stop and reload for a better balance. As the morning wore on, the baking heat was intensified by a parching east wind.

Early in the afternoon, Bib signaled that he wished to leave the room, and I excused him, watching out the window to see that he did not go to the water trough, for we had cool water recently brought from the spring in a bucket beside the door. Though the boy performed willingly and well all tasks assigned him, he liked to wander off when camp chores were finished. This activity should also apply to schoolroom tasks, he reasoned, and I was constantly alerted to his fiddle-foot habits. With no more formal instruction than the others, he read rapidly and accurately with a natural skill, but unless it be a subject that interested him, he made no attempt to link meaning to the printed page. I suspected that, during his glib perusal of assignments, he mentally engaged in fighting Indians, hunting big game, or blazing trails through the wilderness, beset with dangers and surmounting all difficulties with heroic deeds.

I noted that his destination was, indeed, our toilet, for regardless of school law, the school camp afforded only one. It was stoutly built on lines determined by generations of plumbing-less facilities and was, like the school, anchored by cables to rock outcrops. I soon forgot about Bib as classes followed their daily routine.

A sharp crackling, ominous in the dead atmosphere of midday, brought me to my feet in alarm. From the window, I saw the toilet ablaze and caught a fleeting glimpse of a bare-legged child disappearing in a clump of jack pine above the spring. In response to my sharp exclamation, Young Jim and Clem were out sprinting toward the water trough, snatching saddle blankets to souse and beat out the spreading flames.

"Buckets, girls! Quick," I called and ran to get a blanket and the shovel.

Our sanctum was already an inferno, and we made no attempt to save it, attention centering wholly on controlling the rapid progress of fire through dry cheat and weeds. It was perilously close to a thicket of lodge pole pine, from which it would spread into a conflagration of frightening magnitude, wiping out the school camp and burning over thousands of acres of timber—trapping cattle and destroying precious summer range.

"Don't use water for anything but sousing," shouted Young Jim. "We only got what's in the trough, and it runs in slow."

Perceiving the wisdom of this, the girls ran for blankets.

For fully an hour, we battled the stubborn creep of flames, fighting on a dozen fronts. The fringe fires were finally out, and we were exhausted, blackened, and spurting perspiration through every pore. All had burns of some description, and I felt ill with the reaction from the frightening catastrophe we had only narrowly averted. Young Jim approached to shovel dirt on the still angrily blazing remains of our sanctum. Then, and not until then, did we remember Bib, for there, glowing in the embers, were the remains of his boots, charred and curled but still identifiable.

"Bib!" exclaimed Young Jim, gazing wildly around.

For one instant, I knew the absolute of horror as I faced the lad across the glowing ruins. His face was paper white through his tan. Then I remembered that fleeting impression of a half-naked child streaking up the hill.

"I saw him running for the timber," I pointed. "Go after him, Jim. He can't have gone far."

I shepherded the other children to the cook tent, and we washed and received first aid, smearing wet soda on the burns, all minor.

Time passed, and Young Jim did not return. Anger at the graceless Bib, whom I knew to be responsible for this near holocaust, turned to apprehension and then active fear. If his panic at the havoc he had wrought had sent him fleeing wildly into the vast timbered country that led upward from the rims, he might even by this time be hopelessly lost. A lost child in this wild hinterland! Alarmed at the thought, I envisioned days of search—men riding far and wide.

Resolutely, I strove to conquer mounting fear, determined that my feeling of panic should not be communicated to the children. There was work to be done. A resumption of classes was out of the question, a waste of time under the circumstance. We'd have to get up a toilet of sorts. At any cost, the decencies of living must be maintained. The children agreed solemnly that this was so. Clem was dispatched with the shovel for trench work, and I took the ax and proceeded to a stand of young lodge pole, where I hacked industriously, the girls trimming the fallen saplings with pocketknives and the little boys dragging them to the scene of construction near our former sanctum. It was suffocating in the searing heat. We all sweated mightily, our burns and scratches smarting, but we labored on. More than an hour had passed when I saw Young Jim coming down the Rim Trail from the south, alone. My heart raced and skipped a beat as I hurried to meet him.

"I found him," Jim announced. "He doubled back to the Rim Trail, and I tracked him nearly to Pan Creek. He came back aways, and now he won't come no farther. He's up there behind that rock," he said, pointing. "Shoulda knocked him cold and drug him in." He looked a small replica of the elder Jim in his sterner moments.

"But why? Why won't he come?"

"Says he won't come in without no pants."

"Pants!" I exclaimed, controlling an impulse to laugh wildly with pure relief from fear. "What became of his pants, anyway?"

"Burned up along with his boots, I reckon. Know how that fire started?" he continued ominously. "Struck matches to light a cigareet. Stole the tobacco and papers from Dace's pack."

"But his pants. What about his pants?"

"Says he went down there to cool off and took off his pants and boots for a spell. Then he decided to have a cigareet. Says he's no idea how the fire started. Just like that, and the whole shebang was going up in smoke. Tried to beat it out with his pants, and then the pants got afire, so he just dropped them and run. Striking matches and smoking cigareets! Wait till Dad gets hold of him. Bet he won't sit for a week!"

"Get a strip of canvas from the packs," I said. "He'll have to manage it somehow for pants. And then bring him to me at the schoolhouse."

There would be no pants, no shoes, for Bib throughout the week. Our situation did not permit the luxury of a complete change of clothing. The boys donned clean overalls each Monday morning at home, bringing only one clean shirt for change in midweek; the girls had one clean frock. There were no extras.

In grim mood, I awaited the coming of the errant Bib, who had broken the most rigid rule of the camp—the unwarranted striking of a match. Approaching along the trail, the culprit was in the lead being roughly nudged along by Young Jim. Shorn of his brave raiment, he was indeed a sorry figure. The strip of canvas was wound about his hips, sarong fashion, and he had some ado to avoid entanglement in its flapping ends. His shirt was torn and blackened. Barefoot, he limped along like a lost young colt. Young Jim thrust him in the schoolhouse, shut the door firmly, and committed himself to the sanctum construction.

Under my stern gaze, Bib crept hesitatingly, painfully to my desk. Slowly, he raised his eyes. Those bright blue eyes, always so self-reliant, so gay, were filmed with the misery of his guilt and personal degradation. For seconds, he gazed at me pleadingly.

"I didn't go to do it," he whispered, clinging to the desk's edge.

It was then I noted his arms, on which ugly blisters had already formed. His flaxen thatch was singed deeply; one ear and cheek flamed with burn. The canvas hid other painful evidences of his adventure. Quickly I walked to the window to hide a wave of compassion, knowing that, come what might, I could not inflict further physical suffering on this wretched child. But no such gentle compunction was evidenced by the children outside, for I noted that the pace of construction had noticeably slackened. Eyes and ears were alert to what was to transpire in the schoolhouse. Plainly, punishment to fit the enormity of the crime was expected, and I saw myself falling far short as a disciplinarian.

Donning my sternest front, I returned to the waiting child. "Your father will punish as he sees fit," I announced coldly, screening from my voice the deep concern I felt for the smarting flesh and crushed spirit of my most troublesome charge.

Briefly I sketched the scope of his offense. Useless to dwell on the smoking of tobacco, which was regarded by both old and young in this country as only a negligible tool of Satan. Rather, I bore down heavily on the careless use of matches, by which could result such disaster as we had barely escaped that afternoon.

"Come down to the cook tent, and we'll see about those burns," I said at the conclusion of the lecture. "And then you'll get to work with the others. I don't know what you'll do for pants." Then with the malice of youth I added, "I've an extra skirt you can use."

"I can make do with the canvas," he said quickly, scurrying to the door. "Anyway, I still got my hat." Something of the old brightness came into his eyes as he paused beside the monstrous headpiece hung on a nail at the back of the room.

"Won't do much for your bare legs and feet," I commented, irritated that the hat hadn't burned along with the rest of the extraordinary outfit.

He clasped the grotesque affair on his head and preceded me to the cook tent, gathering his canvas about him with an air and discarding the limp for just the faintest hint of a swagger. Bib's spirits had revived miraculously; punishment was deferred, and Friday night presented only a vague threat.

The girls prepared supper unsupervised that evening, and I labored on with the boys. By night, we had up a toilet of sorts. Its interior offered none of the refinements usually featured in that classic of American architecture. Outside it resembled the wickiups, which in later years, I was to note in the camps of the Nez Perce when they streamed into the Salmon River country during hunting season. The slim poles were fitted close in a circular arrangement, their tapering tops gathered together at the apex and tied with a lash rope. The door was hung with a strip of canvas, and as an extra embellishment, the boys had chinked the cracks between the poles with mud. It was an amazing edifice, and we all gathered around to admire our handiwork. But Young Jim's eyes were troubled as he scanned the wide area about us, charred by the remains of our grass fire.

"If any of the forest men come along and see this burn-off, we'll be in trouble for sure," Jim said.

We fell silent under the impact of this new threat. This was forest reserve land, and the school camp was on it through the good graces of the United States Department of Agriculture. It was a privilege not to be treated lightly, and any indication that gross carelessness with fire existed might close the school camp permanently. In any event, there would be questions, endless explanations, embarrassment for the school board, interviews, reports. Always reports. I envisioned myself listed in district forestry records as an irresponsible young person, unfit to supervise children. Inquiries might even filter farther afield and add little glory to my teaching reputation. The thought galvanized me to action.

"Let's try to cover it," I suggested. "Scrape pine needles and dirt over it."

We labored until dark, carrying loads of dirt and pine needles to scatter about. Afterward, we worked by the light of our lantern. But at ten o'clock, hardly half of the area was camouflaged. Agreeing to finish in the early morning before school, we retired, a weary crew, to the cook tent for a before-bed snack of bread and cold boiled beef, plus further treatment of smarting burns, abrasions, and more recently acquired work blisters.

It was far past bedtime for the children, but a task yet remained for me. Bib would have to have pants of some sort. The strip of canvas was a constant aggravation and an impediment to work. So after the others were asleep, I worked by lantern light on the cook tent table, using Young Jim's overalls as a pattern to cut a pair of pants from the canvas strip. I was careful to omit the bib. Unable to cope with the intricacies of a buttoned fly, I fashioned the creation in wrap-around mode with tie strings. The stitching operation was accomplished by means of cord string threaded through a darning needle. Moths bumbled about the light, frequently batting me in the face, and a horde of mosquitoes added their bit to the merriment. Aggravated further by my sore fingers, I heartily regretted not having meted out to Bib the punishment he so richly deserved. It was past midnight when I carried my finished product to the boys' tent, returned to the girls' tent, extinguished the lantern, and retired.

Before the next evening came, Bib had added a dashing accessory to the pants, using scraps of canvas to cut a deep fringe which he sewed with cord down the side of each leg, Indian scout fashion. Thus accoutered, he was quite the old Bib again, playing heroic roles with no apparent apprehension for the fast approaching time of reckoning.

We worked the next morning until school time, instantly fearful lest a ranger should ride by before the task was finished. Even completed and every trace of our blackened area covered, I reflected uneasily that the peculiar edifice we had erected was sufficient to draw the scrutiny of any passerby, forest service or not. For once, we dreaded the appearance of riders. We were constantly alerted to such approaches, but through that entire week, nothing moved along the trail.

The scorching east wind continued, and on Wednesday, our meat was spoiled. Meat was the mainstay of camp menus, and without it, there was general dissatisfaction. Bib brought in half a dozen pine squirrels, and that night we had squirrel stew, which, in spite of my feeling about the matter, I found amazingly tasty.

The searing heat seemed to increase with devilish intensity. There was something ominous about the way it hung on.

A deadly calm settled over the rim country late Thursday afternoon. The noisy blue jays and stealthy camp robbers were hidden and silent; our bevy of gay chipmunks disappeared. All evidence of the small wildlife friendly to our camp went into some sanctuary known only to its kind. Not a leaf stirred.

Our animals were strangely restless as evening came. Old Mouse, turned out for nightly forage, refused to leave the corral and paced back and forth, the horses within, keeping up with her restless movements. The dogs whined, and Jupe left the corral to be close to us. Maxie pressed against my knees as we sat around outside the cook tent. Our usually noisy little group was silent with a nameless sort of apprehension.

Black clouds spun from the Wallowas across the canyon, throwing an early cape of blackness about us. All over the vast canyon country, the silence was as a universal death. An oppressive humidity enveloped us, and we refrained from kindling smudge pots lest an errant spark mate with tinder-dry material. We retired to our quarters as early darkness cloaked the camp. The only creatures abroad that night were the mosquitoes, and they went about their work with ghoulish precision. Drenched with perspiration, I threw off my bunk blankets and dared them to do their worst. Maryadee and Essie tossed in restless slumber, and Maxie panted softly on the floor beside my bunk.

Hours later, I was awakened by the high, thin scream of the wind. A flash of lightning revealed the interior of the tent in an eerie light, the two girls sitting upright in their bunk, eyes round with fright and faces startlingly pale. A roll of thunder shook our frail shelter as I leaped from the bunk, pulling my riding skirt on over my nightdress and groping for my boots and jacket. A storm of peculiar intensity was sweeping the breaks of the canyon. I realized as the wind rose to a higher pitch, shrieking with the concentrated fury of a cosmic bow drawn across countless taut strings, Young Jim was at the door.

"Teacher," he called, his voice thin with urgency, "can you and the girls get your bedding up to the schoolhouse? A branch might fall. It isn't safe here. Quick as you can." In those simple words, command passed to Young Jim.

"Right away," I answered.

We staggered to the schoolhouse under loads of bedding, every step raked by the fury of the wind. I placed the lantern beside me and drew the four children close, impressing on them the importance of not stirring from the shelter. Maryadee collapsed on the bedding and burrowed into it, but the little boys and Essie, pigtails bobbing, stood their ground as a clap of thunder, augmenting the gale, smashed down and the stout building trembled. The cables holding it to the great rocks creaked under the impact of the wrenching attack.

With the lantern, I rushed outside, bidding Essie put props against the door, and fought my way back to the tents to help the boys batten down flaps and tighten ropes, but Clem and Bib were already at the corral, where flashes of lightning revealed our horses milling wildly.

"They're locoed," shouted Young Jim. "That corral will never hold them. Only chance is to get hackamores and snub them up to the posts. We gotta hurry before they break through."

I groped about in our wind-scattered gear for a hackamore, locating one just as the wind tore a branch from the Ponderosa, hurling it on the cook tent. Above the roar of the elements, we heard the crash of utensils as it plummeted through the canvas.

"Quick," Young Jim yelled. "It coulda hit you."

Hackamores in hand, we raced for the corral.

Halfway down the slope, a series of flashes illuminated the canyon of the Snake in a lurid, searching light, magnifying the rimrock on the Idaho side. The clefts and precipices of the guardian Seven Devils glowed. Every crevice, every craggy turret of the demoniac cluster was revealed in such livid splendor that I rocked back, transfixed by the display of unearthly beauty. Then a shutter of blackness swept across it, and I stumbled forward to the job ahead, knowing that, at all costs, the horses must be kept in bounds.

Even to this day, few catastrophes in the precipitous land of the Snake and Salmon can be compared to the loss of one's saddle horse. A person afoot is a derelict indeed. To lose our pack animals and saddle horses at one fell swoop would be a calamity overwhelming. Loosed, the frenzied animals might seep to the rims and destruction, or they might, with better sense, be guided to the home trail of the river ranch. In any event, days of search would be involved to gather them. Old Mouse had already taken off, for flashes revealed no sight of her.

The poles of which the corral was constructed, though sturdy enough for stressless hours, were not designed for the confinement of frenzied beasts. Octagonal in shape, the mainstays of the structure were the eight massive uprights to which the poles were nailed. The job at hand was to get a hackamore on each horse and snub its head up close to one of these posts. Two horses were already thus secured by the time Young Jim and I reached the enclosure.

Climbing to the topmost rail at the post assigned me by Young Jim, I was horrified to see in a flash of light that Bib was in the corral, darting here and there, attempting to move the horses against the poles where Clem or Young Jim could use their ropes and hackamores to advantage. The horses, wall-eyed with terror, raced about the corral, manes and tails streaming in the wind. Bib, clad only in his canvas trousers, brave leg fringes whipping in the gale, was a frail object amid those flying hooves.

"Dear heaven," I moaned, "he'll be killed. Trampled." I screamed, "Jim, get him out of there. Get him out!"

If my frenzied voice was heard above the confusion in the heavens, not the slightest attention was paid me. This was no time for orders from a terrified girl schoolteacher, for these children had known the fierce onslaughts of a relentless land since toddling days. They were reared to emergency, and those unable to cope with situations of the most desperate sort survived only by a miracle. I turned away as the next revealing flash came, conscious of my own futility. Darkness mercifully spared me most of what went on in the corral.

"Here's Riley." It was Clem's voice close by. A hackamore rope was thrust into my hand. "Snub him close up with a double hitch around the post while I hold him." Automatically I did so, recalling only afterward how well I had learned to tie the various knots, which Brick had drilled into my subconscious by insistent practice.

The horses were all secured before the rain came, sweeping down in torrents, drenching me in seconds, and running in streams down my thinly clad body into my boots. Under its chilling impact, the horses quieted. The savage lightning gave way to heat flashes eastward, and the thunder rolled distantly. The wind lulled, but the downpour continued as we clung to our posts, calling to each other, counting growing glows on the Idaho side where lightning had struck and timber was blazing. The horses hunched their streaming backs dispiritedly. There was no fight left in any of them, and we removed the hackamores.

Wearily we straggled back to the school, a gray outline in the wet dawn. The children had fallen asleep in the jumble of bedding, and the three exhausted boys threw themselves down on blankets and straightway slumbered in their wet clothes. I sat for a long time on a bench, dazed by fatigue, wondering if I should extract a blanket from the mess and find a corner for myself.

Instead I stepped out on our little porch to see that light was coming fast in a fair eastern sky. Sodden, disheveled, and dog-tired, I gazed about our camp, desolate in the half-light. The rain had ceased, and the trees dripped sadly. A great hole was torn in the cook tent, and I envisioned with a shudder the disorder and waste within. The boys' quarters appeared intact, but the girls' tent had been ripped from its frame and trailed dismally from its rear ropes. Visions of a change to dry clothes vanished. Everything I possessed would be as soaked as the sorry raiment on my back. Our saddles and packing gear, all as wet as if they had been immersed, added to the damage inflicted on saddle blankets during the fire fighting. Our wickiup sanctum had been completely removed from the scene with only scattered poles and drenched debris to show for all our work. There was slight comfort in the fact that the general disorder had covered all traces of our fire, for it already seemed of little consequence compared to the overall havoc.

I sat down weakly on the porch steps, gazed dully at the wreckage, and decided that this summer's term would be ended by the catastrophe. Maxie, who had never left me during that whole wretched night, capered foolishly, showering me with residue from his wet coat, and displayed an animated interest in life that I was far from sharing. He was the first to hear the hoof beats approaching from the north. There were at least two riders, I decided, and they were riding fast in spite of half-light and a heavy trail. I started up, conscious that I was still clad partially in nightdress and that I was soaked, muddy, and wholly unfit to be seen.

But when the first rider rounded the turn leading down the draw to the school, and I recognized the familiar grace of the tall man in the saddle, I ran forward to meet him, crying with relief, "Pat! Oh, Pat! I'm so glad, so glad ..."

Swinging down, he caught me, and I crumpled against his chest. It was the most satisfactory crumpling spot I had known for a good, long time, and I cared not a whit that Jim Garrter, following close behind, witnessed the total collapse of professional dignity. Through the years, I recall no occasion when the appearance of the male of the species so imbued me with all-out surrender of responsibility. Just their presence assured me that the wrenching wounds of the school camp would be bound up and that, by means of patches, props, and pluck, we would carry on.

For in spite of injuries from storm and fire, repairs would be made. Brands scattered far from their grazing areas would be gathered. Trails would be cleared. The forest service would move in with long pack trains to battle lightning-set fires. Young aspen, beaten to the earth, would rise again, and with patient fortitude the wounds of the ponderosa would eventually heal.

To pick up and go on, to survive against perpetual struggle, is the law of this enduring river country. Deep in its canyons, steadfastness is its substance, and deep is the spirit of its people to continue.

28

The Battle for Water

The struggle to utilize the water of the Snake began nearly a century ago. Along its stately sweep through the sagebrush plains of southern Idaho, the effort was resolved by building low dams to generate power and transfer the slumbering desert to lush fields of alfalfa and potatoes.

It was in a lower section between Lewiston and the foot of Hells Canyon where the canyon widens that the grimmest battle for water took place. It became an epic struggle on a local plane and, in recent years, has developed into a national hassle because a new factor entered the picture. Power. Who is to develop it and how?

In this section, the settlers' first encounter with the Snake was not waged on the basis of power, a force then in its infancy. Rather, the lift of water was sought to irrigate alluvial bars and bench land, where pioneers had established the nucleus of cattle and sheep dynasties. Though meagerly treated by historians, this struggle continued for over fifty years and is one of the dramatic episodes of the West.

Evidence of the battle is still in the wreckage of instruments these people employed to gain water, but few are now left who can explain their meaning or the forces that motivated the effort.

Today, flying up the Snake from Lewiston toward Hells Canyon, the casual observer looks down on small river bars and upper benches, many of them less than fifty acres. One wonders why men should have toiled a lifetime and spent fortunes in trying to raise water to such meager patches.

The answer lies in altitudes, terrains, and early methods of stock raising. The latter is now history, but the rugged country is the same; the drastic climatic changes from rims to river remain constant and still present nature's forces in the new battle for power and flood control.

The cattle industry here between the 1880s and the third decade of the new century followed the pattern of open range, but to use such range, a man must have a substantial foothold on the river. Key positions were taken early. They commanded a river bar or several upper benches where alfalfa or other winter feed could be raised and cattle wintered at a minimum of loss.

Range fell into three belts—winter range and feed lots on the river; spring and fall range extending up the mountain sides from 1,000 to 2,500 feet elevation; and summer range "on top," where cattle roamed over the forest reserve and beef was finished for market. It was a range cycle repeated year after year, and on it, early cattle fortunes were built.

The critical months were those on the river, for who knew

when a hard winter would hit, when snow would come to the water's edge and haystacks would be quickly diminished? The amount of hay that a cattleman could muster and the extent of his winter range, therefore, controlled the size of his herd and his fortune.

No river bar, no low elevation bench was too small to be ignored in the struggle to accumulate winter feed. If supplied with irrigation, as many as five cuttings of alfalfa could be had off these river canyon acres, and fifty acres on the river were worth more than two hundred at higher elevations. Hay was hoarded, like gold, and held over if possible from year to year, though after three years, mice and weather largely destroyed its vitality. A store of hay in any shape was insurance against the specter of a hard winter.

The struggle to possess irrigable land at the lowest possible altitude was the aim of every man who longed for the prestige of a big outfit.

Often a creek with a year-round flow, plunging down its own steep canyon to the Snake, could be tapped and its water flumed or ditched around mountains to these precious hay fields. Where nature offered no such rewards, a man, though his river holdings boasted a hundred acres of hay land, sat on a "dry ranch," and he could only brood on the steady, mocking flow of the Snake and plot means to bring a small portion of its immense volume to his arid ground.

Often the efforts of these unfortunate ones became obsessions pursued with fanatic intensity. One man who possessed a fine bar of more than sixty acres, spent forty years digging a tunnel in the steep hill above his home. He heard running water and constantly expected to strike a living vein. Ironically, what he heard was the echo of the Snake, and though this was suggested to him many times, he still dug doggedly until his death in pursuit of an echo. The murmur of the river at the face of his tunnel can be heard to this day.

Another man of inventive nature spent years constructing a giant wooden windmill, which never raised a drop of water. He is now gone, and a power pump raises water from the Snake. Its pipeline to his bar crosses the decaying wreckage of the mill.

Another fellow lived alone on a tiny bar in one of the most formidable sections of the canyon. He owned six acres, which he irrigated from a spring, but unlike the others, he had no aspirations to raise hay and tend cattle. He raised peaches.

Stockmen coveted his holdings as a location for small winter feed grounds and made him flattering offers, which he refused. His bar was known to be one of the richest placer sites on the river, and mining concerns made fabulous bids for placer rights. These he likewise scorned.

The old man serenely raised peaches, and his activities became a legend on the river, for he converted most of his prized fruit into a very fine brandy, eagerly sought by the riding fraternity. When he needed clothes or staple groceries, he carelessly panned out some gold dust and sent it down the river on the mail boat to Lewiston, along with a list of his modest needs.

29

Beef Tally

For the three days of the roundup, summer drew a final breath, holding it in a cosmic pause before expelling dreary portents of harsh days to come. The high meadows lay in a soft haze. The dusty drench of pine and sere grasses brewed with lean atmosphere and thin, golden sunshine. Like a nebulous veil it lay over the canyon of the Snake, blurring the severity of brown slopes and barren rims. Dusty shades of mauve dulled the jagged horizon of the Seven Devils, rolling on eastward to the land of the Bitter Root, south to the Sawtooth. Westward the Wallowas ran in rock veins up to the grandeur of Eagle Cap and Sacajawea Peak.

Dwarfed by this ageless magnificence, man went about his trivial activities working in a minute segment of space and time. His cattle moved on to the high meadows from all over the vast summer ranges. Herds to be returned to fall forage were cut out from beef and, after branding and marking, were started on their way down the lower Snake slopes. The cattle were held on the meadows by means of short stretches of drift fence, augmented by riders who worked in four shifts from dawn to dawn. Brands were tallied, and there were endless conclaves between cattlemen and beef buyers. All worked to a final climax—the starting of the long cattle drive across the canyon-cut northern foothills of the Wallowas to the shipping pens at Enterprise.

"Every year this time, them two rakes talk poor old crazy Sugar out of sugar and make up a mess of pizen moonshine, bring it up here to the roundup, an' peddle it for good money. It's a hard-enough time for all of us without our menfolk sickin' themselves on that filth."

Bess Garrter glared at the two rakes, Lava Pete and Chance Micksel, who had paused some distance from our camp for an overall survey of roundup activities. They were indeed an uncouth pair. Lava, sooty-bearded and clad in a shabby flannel shirt, dark vest, and angora chaps, kept his black felt pulled well down over his eyes. His younger companion, a slight youth with pimply face and darting eyes, was badly in need of barbering service.

Bess began to curse conversationally and throw packing gear about.

"I don't see how they ever induced that old man to part with any of his sugar," I said.

"Got him drunk, of course, and then just helped themselves, the danged skunks," said Bess. "'Twouldn't be so bad if it was good whiskey. But that pizen stuff they brew up, it scalds a man's insides. Pantherpee, the boys call it, and that's namin' it mild."

The two dissolute ones, evidently feeling themselves under fire, moved slowly toward the work corrals, trailed by their packhorses.

"Know better, they do, than to unload that pack around here," snorted Bess. "There's enough straight-shootin' women in camp to bust them jugs in a couple of shots. But you can't go shootin' at a horse critter. 'Taint it's fault it's a carryin' that rotgut."

I thought it too bad that the whiskey problem should be introduced on this, the first day of the roundup, and I should have enjoyed seeing Bess make a target of the noxious pack, but Lava Pete and Chance showed no inclination to unload and moved steadily along toward the big meadow, where a cloud of dust was being stirred by hundreds of milling cattle.

We were camped in an old corral whose log timbers were disintegrating from age. It was the first of the massive corrals built in the area, a familiar landmark known far and wide as Hepps Corral, presumably for reasons of association with its builder. It must have been more than fifty years old at this time, and it was, traditionally, the campsite for the roundup, the big work corrals having been more recently built over on the edge of the meadow.

No one could tell me for how many years the families of the stockmen had participated in the roundup, but its general routine proved it a long-established custom. It was picnicking on a grand scale; it was all the year's holidays in one. It was the only annual get-together of the river clans, and it afforded the only official holiday of the term, school being dismissed Thursday at noon so that we might participate.

Hepps Corral had been a packing station in early times. About fifty feet in diameter, it had once been a formidable structure. Scarred now by time and hard usage, its top logs had been tumbled off, and those below were merging into each other through decay. The rotting wood sifted to the ground in cinnamon-brown dust.

The only remaining building of the historic station was near the corral entrance. Originally of log construction, it had a hand-hewn floor of unbelievable thickness. After abandonment of the station, the walls of the building had been torn away and a steep, shake-covered roof was supported by great log uprights at each corner. Here we danced. The floor, though worn down by the elements and the shuffling of booted feet, was still the roughest I have ever trod.

Centering Hepps Corral was the barbecue pit, and it too showed evidence of long use. There was a long, hand-hewn table along one side, for eating at the roundup was communal. Outside of the roasting of a prime steer, little cooking was done, each family bringing food already prepared from the home camp.

We placed our bedrolls along the corral wall, and Bess and I fastened tarps from the top log, extending them out over light pole frames to afford shade during the day. At night, the tarps were slanted down to stakes beside the bedrolls, thus providing some slight privacy for slumber.

In this manner, the families were afforded camp facilities within Hepps Corral, and there was additional space for guest bedrolls.

Allie and the kids arrived, squired into camp by Estie, who had met them at the fork of the Rim Trail. Proudly he rode into camp followed by the Raber cavalcade. With the memory of the hazardous way from the river to the rims still strong within me, I stared incredulously and then shuddered at what I saw.

Following Estie was a patient packhorse with their eldest, a boy of eight, astride the sawbuck packsaddle. In the alforjas slung on each side were packing cases, and each case held two children, ranging in size down the stair steps of their family. One tiny child and an older one had been placed in each case, not only for required balance but also as a supervisory expedient. They gazed happily about them with wondering eyes.

Next came Allie with the infant, which lay in a sling about her shoulders. They were massive shoulders, and Allie was a massive girl. She overflowed the saddle in every direction. Two pack mules laden with food and camp gear trailed the procession.

"Want you to get to know Allie and the kids real well." The diminutive Essie beamed. "Guess we'll camp right alongside you, eh, Allie?"

Donna Trelschmeir and I perched on the top log of the big corral along with a score of other spectators, watching the activities therein. Riders were cutting in the meadow and hazing calves into the corral. The soft September air was slashed with the odor of seared flesh and scorching hair.

"Dave Bolter's pretty handy with his rope," I observed. "He never misses a throw."

"Cows!" exclaimed Donna. "All he knows. All he'll ever know." I heard the whipping scorn in her voice.

"My last roundup," said Donna. "It's my turn to go out to school this fall, and when I go this time, I'll never come back."

"You have everything here," I said, recalling that the brand most frequently seen on the high range was that of her father.

"You think so?" A flush had crept under the smooth tan of the girl's cheeks and throat. Her gray eyes smoldered under straight, black brows. "Actually, we're broke, and that's a fact. Have been ever since I can remember. Ever wonder why Dean and I have taken turns going out to school? And when I do go, I can't have clothes like the other girls?"

"You could have your pick of any man in this country," I said, mentally reserving Pat.

"That would be just jake, wouldn't it?" She laughed derisively. "What a choice! This river is the end for a woman," Donna went on. "Maybe you won't believe it, but I can remember when Bess Garrter was a good-looking girl. Look at her now! Sure, she can run a pack string good as any man. Sure, she can shoe a horse, shoot straight, and ride over these hellish trails with the best of them. Cook, wash, scrub, and sew. Raise four kids while doing all that. But I've seen how women live on the outside, and this devil's canyon trap isn't for me."

Mrs. Mac, who had undertaken general policing of the children, was determined that there should be ice cream for them, and Justin MacDeen had no peace until a rider and packhorse were dispatched to the old Coffin Creek Mine where ice lay in its tunnel the year-round. A good portion of the pack load melted in route.

A mixture of cornstarch custard, condensed milk, and flavoring was placed in a lard bucket and twirled by the bail in a receptacle filled with ice and stock salt. The women took turns at the churning operation, and after more than an hour of effort, we turned out a coarse slush, which the youngsters hailed with shouts of joy. The wonder and delight of the little Rabers was something to see. It was their first ice cream.

"Hardly civilized, are they?" remarked Drum, the cattle buyer from Spokane who stood by, hands in pockets, watching the children who had polished off the cream and were now battling for possession of the ice chunks.

"Not if you figure that ice cream is an essential mark of civilization," I returned tartly, observing with distaste this person, Drum. What his real name was, I never knew. He was the over fleshed product of soft living, and he looked completely out of place here. The stockman's garb he affected was alien to him.

"How'd a nice-looking girl like you happen to get stuck in this jumping off place?" His tone was intimate, patronizing, and his shallow eyes roved over my scuffed boots, my patched khaki skirt and blouse, now nearly white from many washings.

"I was reared on this river, and I am not stuck here," I replied.

"Well now," his tone became silky, "you surely get to Spokane or Lewiston occasionally, and when you do—"

"I don't, and I won't," I interrupted rudely and walked away.

Why was their music so sad? No lilting gaiety, only a melancholy wailing in the old folk tunes. A trio of fiddles, harmonicas, and an accordion comprised the roundup orchestra.

Pat and I danced.

Merriment there was in generous measure, but since a good number of the country's young bloods were doing their fighting on the fields of France, much of the traditional brawling was absent. As the evening progressed, frequent drags from fraternal jugs heightened masculine spirits. The music struck a faster tempo but with the same nostalgic undertones. Pat and I danced on. He had been drinking, but not too much.

Dace Bolter had had much too much drink and was forgetting his studied role of womanhater. In the dull light of lanterns hung from crossbeams, I could see that he was giving the tall, blond girl from Lewiston quite a line.

Pat laughed. "Not so dead set on kidding himself tonight," he said.

Pat was due on herd duty at midnight, so we left the dance and strolled over to the barbecue pit. With meat between slabs of bread and tin cups of bitter black coffee, we sat on our bedrolls by the Garrter fire.

"Time's running out here," said Pat. "This time tomorrow night, I'll be on the trail with the lead herd. Final destination, France."

"You'll come back, Pat," I whispered, my cheek against his shoulder.

"I sure as hell aim to, Girl," he said.

Standing beside Lucky out on the meadow trail, we said our tender goodbyes, for the confusion of the morrow gave no hope of intimate moments. Held in our hearts for many months were the promises of that parting, but human relations are transitory, and youth particularly is spendthrift with companionship, dissipating its permanence in new scenes, new pleasures.

There was visible promise of a new day, but less than half of the crowd slept. The others milled about. Plaintive music still came from the dance floor. Groups talked and ate about the barbecue. Others squatted around the fires that formed an inner circle of brightness about the corral and marked the headquarters of a family or group. There were twelve such fires, constantly replenished against the chill of approaching dawn.

The fame of the historic roundup had attracted some thirty adventurous souls from points outside—some from

Lewiston, some from the range country of the Idaho side, and others from Oregon's Imnaha and the Grande Ronde. There were three cattle buyers from metropolitan marts, welcomed by the stockmen for business reasons, plus the usual supply of good liquor they brought along to facilitate transactions.

Food there was in abundance, but meals as such were not served. When hungry, people sought portions of the savory roast beef, helped themselves from the array of grub boxes set up beside the long table, and washed their cup and plate at the water trough near the corral entrance. When exhausted, a person located his or her bedroll, and it was bad manners to appear irked if it was found to be already occupied, since a number of roundup guests had come without blankets. Each person utilized anyone's food, dishes, or bedrolls, and since only a few ate or slept at the same time, it usually worked out. It was, however, no place for the finicky-minded.

Bess had succeeded in guarding my bed from intruders, and I decided to crawl under the tarp for a predawn nap when Danny Durst strolled over, resplendent in all his dude ranch finery. His effrontery in this matter went unchallenged at the roundup, since a number of outside guests had come decked out in rodeo regalia, and to subject Danny to the usual humiliations would have likewise discredited the visitors, who doubtless felt they were correctly garbed for the occasion. So, Danny swaggered with impunity, and I was glad that he was getting away with his brief triumph. The boy had suffered enough. Furthermore, the brilliant shirts and neckerchiefs of the few provided a gay accent among the soberly garbed working stockmen and added a note of festivity to the occasion.

"Only had three dances this whole night. Not enough women to go around, and I could never even get near enough to ask you while Pat was around." There was a wistfulness in Danny's voice.

I was dog-tired, and my feet ached miserably from dancing on that frightful floor, but for Danny, whom I considered had been wretchedly treated all summer, I would rise again and dance until dawn. Under the lad's oafishness there was innate kindness, and I had to admit that he was, for all his vagaries, behaving with more dignity on this occasion than were his self-elected superiors.

"Are they still dancing?" I asked, feigning interest.

"Sure are," he responded eagerly. "They'll dance right along till daylight.

"Well then, what are we waiting for?" I cried, springing up.

There was a brief respite for the stock dogs during the roundup, but throughout the preceding two weeks when cattle were gathered from the rugged draws and rocky creek canyons, their work was indispensable. It was the most difficult of all the year's work on horses and men, but particularly was it hard on the dogs, for they were sent into the more impenetrable sections to scout out stock hidden by thickets of jack pine and chaparral.

During the days of meadow activity, the dogs lay about their masters' camps in Hepps Corral in varying stages of exhaustion, their feet bruised and cut, their bodies emaciated. They slept most of the time, utterly spent, waking only to eat, lap up large quantities of water, and lick their cruelly injured pads. The condition of the dogs had deeply concerned me since the first day of the roundup.

Maxie showed no inclination to follow me about, as was his custom, but lay beside my bedroll and small satchel, leaving them only for brief periods. His attitude was fearful, his soft brown eyes pleading and apologetic. Plainly, the memory of past harsh days was recalled by these surroundings, and he chose my possessions as his only haven of safety.

Trace, Jim Garrter's shepherd, lay by the Garrter campfire, her coat dusty and matted with burrs, and her sleep was like that of death.

"She'll come out of it," said Jim in answer to my anxious inquiries. "A few days of rest, and she'll be able to go on with the beef."

"Isn't there anything to be done for their feet?" I asked.

"They'll heal up in time," said Jim. "Used to be an old feller run cattle here in early days. Old Man Dart—remember him, Bess? Well, he used to make boots out of buckskin for his dogs. Smeared them inside with mutton tallow and laced them on with thongs. Learnt his dogs to wear 'em too. Got to be quite a joke, Old Man Dart and his dog boots."

The peaches that Pittsy Mather raised on his tiny bar near

the mouth of No-Name Creek were no less famous in the canyon country than Pittsy himself. He bestowed his treasures on all at the roundup, passing them out one by one. On the last day, he arrived riding an ancient cavalry saddle on a shambling mare and leading by a rope his packhorse laden with peaches and nothing else. Each fruit had been lovingly wrapped in several thicknesses of newspaper to prevent bruising.

"Some folks calls him crazy, but he's not," Bess told me. "He squats on that danged bar and raises peaches, an' nobody but the Lord-a-mighty'll ever move him offen it. It's the richest little placer spot on the river, but he won't see his peach orchard tore up by no placer minein'. A San Francisco outfit offered him fifty thousand fer that little bit o' ground, but Pittsy just laughs at 'em. He pans out some dust and nuggets now and then fer grub and clothes, but outside that, he's got no time fer nothin' but his peaches. An' fer that, they call him crazy!

"Poor old feller," she continued. "One o' these days, he'll get the call, an' they'll be at his trees like a pack o' varmints."

We strolled over to him.

"Want you to meet our schoolma'am," Bess said.

Pittsy said he was pleased to know me. The reedy voice matched his shriveled person, but the black eyes that appraised me from under brushes of white brows still had snap and fire. Immediately, he reached into his pack and withdrew a peach. Tenderly he unwrapped it, holding it for a moment like a jewel before passing it to me.

I admired its deep golden hue, its downy surface and delicate aroma. It was indeed luscious fruit, deep gold through to the pit. I praised its qualities, and Pattsy beamed.

"Feed on gold, them peaches," he chirped. "That's what gives them the color. And they get that flavor from the syringa blooming on both sides of my little strip. None of them blights and insects can get at my peaches. Too far away from sick trees, they are. At bloom time, they're a sight to behold, and in the fall—well, you see! I like my gold a'growing, making joy for me all the year. Wouldn't like it lying around in a musty, old bank. No, siree, I like it best picking it off of trees."

30

Passage Out

The final two weeks of school following the roundup dragged slowly to a close. Summer was gone, and the coming of gray days set the summer camps in motion to sweep all stock from the high country, close the camps, and trek back to the warmth of river homes. During those raw days, wraiths of mist swirled and broke about the rims. Blue horizons were wiped away. The Seven Devils lay coldly desolate, capped with clouds, and Maxie and I trudged no more to our sunrise communion on the rim.

Pat was gone. Excepting a letter from him at Camp Lewis, our romantic summer was only a memory. Life had turned desolate, and I lived the closing days of the term counting the hours until my departure. Ice had to be broken each morning in the water trough for our pre-breakfast ablutions, and with the bleakly damp and chilly days, a deep nagging ache settled in my old knee injury.

On the last Friday, we stayed the night at the school camp, we worked until noon to store equipment in the schoolhouse and attended to chores that would facilitate the final packing operation. Riding away that gloomy Saturday afternoon, I would not look back at the turn of the trail, shrinking from the final image of our school camp, half dismantled, stark and deserted—left to the fierce onslaughts of approaching winter.

On the Rim Trail for the last time, the joy of my long-anticipated exodus began to fade. For more than a year, I had known no existence beyond the most rigorous, but now plainly visible were the finer points of life "outside," and uneasiness replaced eager longing. In this connection, the condition of my almost nonexistent wardrobe obsessed me, and the tattered state in which I would arrive in Lewiston on the riverboat *Idaho* the following Wednesday, became a matter of grave concern. Fourteen months ago, in that river city, I had boarded the train for Grangeville with brave new luggage, jauntily clad and eager to bring the gospel of suburbia to the hinterland. It now appeared that I, not the hinterland, had been on the receiving end of that mission; its impact, while doubtless good medicine for my brash, young spirit, had proved rough on the material side.

My treasured tricotine suit and accompanying accessories had been reduced to debris during the shattering storm, the suit shrunken to the point where no amount of pressing could restore its original dimensions. For headgear, I had a choice—a shabby tamo'shanter or a felt hat, stained and broken around the crown. Even my jacket, now my only wrap, was in a state bordering on disintegration, as were my threadbare riding skirt and high-top laced boots, scuffed and turned up at the toes. I pictured the amused and pitying stares of the townsfolk trained on me in this dreadful ensemble. A wild-looking young person, lugging a battered satchel and heeled by a small, crippled dog, the latter perchance to be carried in the arms, depending on his reaction to the strange urban clatter.

Maxie was going to be a problem in transit and the final pathetic accent to my scarecrow appearance. Under the influence of this fantastic mental cartooning, I decided therewith to leave Maxie on the river. I had already divided my few books and trinkets among the children, for I was determined to ride out of Hells Canyon without a pack. Abandoning Maxie, therefore, I should have nothing but the clothes on my back, my small satchel, and a pocketful of uncashed checks and school warrants, the latter comforting mainly as a medium of exchange for fashionable attire. Such are the impulses of youth—the fierce desire to conform, to be one of the crowd. But I was yet to discover that the canyon had left its mark and that, deep down inside, much of the willful child was gone forever.

I am convinced that dogs read the minds of humans, particularly their masters. Maxie knew almost as soon as I made my decision to discard him. Of that I am convinced, for he redoubled his efforts to keep me constantly in sight at the Garrter camp. His eyes followed my slightest move; his regard for my few visible belongings was pathetically attentive, and he frequently rested his head on my knee to study me intently.

It was Monday night, and autumn wind stabbed through the ponderosas, knife-edged and vicious with promise of storm. Bess Garrter and I huddled over the cook stove in the summer camp kitchen, mindful of the chilly draft that swept through unchinked cracks in the log wall, flaring the flame of the bracketed oil lamp and etching a crescent of soot on its chimney. We were alone, the children having departed the previous afternoon with Estie Raber, who was packing the last of the equipment to the river. Estie was the final rider to return from the cattle drive, with the exception of Jim Garrter, who, Estie explained diffidently, was planning to come just as soon as he got "some business straightened out." I noted that Bess received that news with anxiety.

Having had a sufficient dosage of the children's company, I sent my satchel down in one of the packs and elected to stay with Bess at the camp, planning to ride with her and Jim to the river in time to take the Wednesday boat. As night closed in and Jim did not come, I sensed my companion's increasing restlessness. We were very much alone on the rim that night. The MacDeens had packed out the school camp equipment, closed their summer camp, and departed for winter quarters. The Bolter camp was deserted, as was the Trelschmeirs', and the feeling of being isolated in a great void obsessed me. The deepening anxiety of Bess Garrter, I knew, did not stem from any physical fear. She had faced that too often. It was something else. Something concerning Jim. Something vital. I longed to know but dared not ask.

Another sound, seeping through the door crack, vied with the mournful symphony in the pine tops. It was Maxie whining softly outside.

"About Maxie," I said hesitatingly. "I can't very well take him with me—on the boat and all. Could you, would you, look after him?" It was a cowardly evasion, and Bess Garrter knew it. Her level gaze told me so.

"We can try," she said. "But he'll pine hisself to death. He's not our kind of dog anymore."

This I knew, for the dogs of the river country were not pets. They were workers. To fondle a stock dog was to destroy his usefulness, according to the stockman's code. Thus, Maxie, severed by affliction from his destined function, was further isolated by human affection, my affection. The whine at the door suddenly became sharp, poignant on a sobbing breath, and the wretched fantasy I had conjured up for Maxie and me on city streets was dispelled.

"What am I thinking of?" I cried. "Of course, I'll take him with me!" Saying it, I knew there could then be no compromise. When you told Bess Garrter you'd do a thing, it was taken as a solemn obligation to be fulfilled at whatever cost to pride or convenience.

At my words, there was a snuffling from outside and a short, sharp bark.

"He knows," said Bess.

"You've done a sight with our younguns this summer," she said. "You learned'em to read real good. That first night you come to the school camp, I knowed you'd top out all right. Her simple words cheered, me for "topping out" to these people meant reaching a distant and always difficult goal.

"It was a pretty good summer, after all," I said.

"We wish you would come back next year. I hoped you wouldn't never leave. If you and Pat ..." She paused.

"I might not have," I said, "but the war changes everything."

There was a sudden, violent outburst of barking from Maxie.

Someone's coming," I said. "It must be Jim."

We waited, listened intently. There was no sound but the rush of wind and Maxie's excited outcries.

"No," said Bess. "Maxie wouldn't bark that away for Jim, ner for any of our folks."

I felt a skin prickle and quickening apprehension. Who would be traveling these deserted rims at night, with all the camps closed and stock off the high range? The men, all but Jim, were back from the drive. The ranger stations were closed for the season. Who could possibly have any business riding to our camp that night? Who but Jim?

Bess stalked to the door, opened it, and stepped outside. A blast of wind swept the room, nearly extinguishing the light. Quickly she returned, shielded the lamp chimney with her palm, and blew out the flame. Instinctively I knew she had then moved to the corner where the .30-30 rifle stood.

"Someone's comin'," Bess said calmly. "I don't know who but not Jim."

She went to the window, a faint blob of gloom against the blackness.

"What do you suppose—" I broke off as a twig from the

ponderosa hit the roof with a sharp crack. I began to shiver violently.

"It's spittin' snow," Bess remarked conversationally. "Just a prowlin' squall likely. Too early for a big blow."

My heart was beating with fast, suffocating throbs. I was, by this time, thoroughly frightened and in no way interested in the weather. I crouched in the darkness, unconsciously massaging my aching knee. Maxie's barking continued, veering to a frenzied pitch. Someone, something was now very near.

"Who can it be?" I whispered.

My answer was a hello from without, the familiar sound of iron striking stone, and the faint clink of bit chains.

"Well," said Bess moving again to the door. "We'll soon find out."

It was Ranger Downey. I recognized his hearty voice immediately and lighted the lamp. He stepped in, casting aside his poncho and felt cap.

"Jim phoned from Joseph this afternoon," he said. "Lucky he caught me. I was just ready to pull out from the station. Buttoning her up for the winter."

"What'd Jim want?" Bess demanded brusquely.

"He's wanting you to ride out to Joseph to meet him. Right away," said Downey. "Something to sign. Says it's important."

Silence in the dimly lighted room. Small particles of sleety snow drove against the window. The moan in the pines rose to a higher pitch. No word was spoken, no sign given. But I knew, and Ranger Downey knew, that Bess Garrter had taken a hard blow. Shadows from the lamp etched her face in a bleak pattern of planes. Something to sign!

Like rock, I thought. Rock of the river, destined ever to punishment—to take it without flinching. Strong, like the rock, and real. One to hold a man's faith. Something to sign!

Bess stepped to the stove, stoked it with energy, and shoved the coffeepot to the front lids.

"You'd better stay the night here," she said. "There's extra blankets in the big room and a passel of grain for your horse. You can turn in the near corral with Riley and Roamer.

"Nix," said Downey. "I've got to get back tonight. Left my packhorse standing. 'Less there's some way I can help by staying."

"You can't help," said Bess, and her face still had that stony look. "Set up and have some grub if you gotta ride back to the station tonight."

She placed cold biscuits and a pan of brown beans on the table, poured three cups of coffee. We sat drinking the hot liquid while Downey ate, talking in his friendly manner about his plans for the winter at forestry headquarters in Missoula.

"You riding to Joseph tomorrow?" he finally queried.

"Yes," said Bess flatly. Her tone implied that further questions were unwelcome.

She turned to me. "Think you can make it to the river ranch alone?"

I assured her that I could.

"That Riley horse, he'll be headed for home," said Downey. "He'll get her there all right."

We went out with Downey—stood while he tightened his saddle cinch. He shook my hand. "Reckon I won't be seeing you again," he said. He paused uncertainly and then said, "Goodbye, Mrs. Garrter—and good luck."

It was as Bess had said, a prowling squall. The stars now shone frostily between scudding clouds. The light snow crunched under our tread.

"Pretty nice of him to ride clear down here from the ranger station," I said.

"Downey's a right decent feller," Bess observed, "for a government man."

We went about our small chores, for the changed plans necessitated an early morning start. Bess had little to say, and I was numbly silent, feeling her desolation. The snow had sifted through the cracks of my lean-to-room, lying in white furrows across the tarp bunk covering. I brushed it off and crept shivering under the blankets. Maxie snuggled at my feet. I thought of Bess. Bess, who had run pack trains, cooked, scrubbed, washed on a board, mended shabby clothes, shoed horses, born and reared children. Bess, who must ride tomorrow in and out of the gorges of the Imnaha and Sheep Creeks, over the rugged Wallowa foothills—to sign something, the prospect of which had turned her face to blank stone.

War demands had brought up beef prices that fall, and there was rejoicing among stockmen. What could it be that Bess must sign? I remembered Mrs. Mac's derisive statements: "The banks own them, lock, stock, and barrel. Jim's good-hearted but is no manager—can't pay off mortgages with that kind of business."

Was Jim in so deep that the now brightening fortunes of the cattle world came too late? Did Estie's evasive manner indicate a poker game, played for high stakes? What must Bess sign?

I was never to know the exact nature of the Garrter's misfortune. Weeks later, Pat wrote me that "Jim had plunged once too often" and that he felt sorry for Bess and the kids, especially Bess, starting again from scratch on a leased ranch. Lying there that night, I considered the impact of this land on the women I had known best—Lydia Sanson, who withdrew from it to inner life; Bess Garrter, who accepted and managed her place in it; Mrs. Mac, who worried at it, terrier-like; and lovely Donna Trelschmeir, who fled from it, defeated.

My last dawn on the rims was bleakly cold with torn veils of mist swirling low. It was barely light when we breakfasted on hotcakes, beans, and coffee. Saddling our horses at the corral, fingers quickly numbed. I wore an old mackinaw, selected from the stock of cast-off garments in the big room. My tam was pulled down over my ears.

"Down aways you'll be sheddin' that mackinaw," said Bess. "It's plenty warm still, on the river."

It was a trail I had never ridden, and she rode out to the breaks with me, stopping where my way veered off sharply to follow a rock wall.

"From here on, it's straight down," she said. "Five hours to the river if you step along. You can't get off the trail. I'll be sayin' so long."

Incredibly clad, she towered above me on her black gelding, Roamer. Chaps encased her long legs, and from an old stag shirt, much too short in the sleeves, her big-boned hands and wrists protruded, red with cold. Carelessly flung across the saddle in front of her was a soiled yellow slicker, and a man's shapeless felt hat was jammed on her head. Ropelike ends of tawny hair sprayed out from the coil at her neck. But in her eyes, in her face, there was repose. Peaceful—passive, like rock. My eyes followed hers across the canyon to the Idaho side, where, momentarily, the mist swirled away and sunlight strafed a patch of rimrock with umber and gold.

"Goodbye, Bess," I said, my voice not too steady.

In response to the reins on his neck, Riley turned eagerly down the trail, and Maxie gave a short, joyous bark. Swiftly we sank into the harsh declivity, and far horizons were lost.

At the first switchback, I turned to look again. Bess still sat there, tall and straight in her saddle, and on my memory, was indelibly engraved that last sight of her—the unforgettable, the essential woman of this eternal frontier. She raised her arm in a wide salute. I answered with like gesture, and the rock of the rims rose between us.

Afterword

Canyon Odyssey

Most great rivers partake of wilderness and taste of many states. They cross humankind's temporal boundaries with impunity; themselves form state and national lines; and savor of folk life, urban and rural, and of work, pastoral and mechanical. Not so the Salmon. It is Idaho's own water, and all the countless streams that cut to its stone channel are the state's own. It coils through mile-deep canyons, and no city mars the primitive integrity of its four hundred-mile sweep. Frontier settlements all; wide places in the trail.

A consistent work pattern marks its course—mines and cattle. From its birth in the lofty Sawtooth peaks and past the Pahsimeroi on to the evil stretches of Snow Hole Rapids and the rugged walls of Blue Canyon at its union with the Snake, it follows the traditional work line.

Other waters, too, are Idaho's own—the Clearwater and its impressive tributaries; the Lochsa and Selway, rising in peaks of the great primitive area and flowing through intermittent canyons and alluvial bars to join the Snake at Lewiston; and, ultimately, the mighty Columbia.

Wildlife slants to these rivers. In the Salmon's upper course, a mountain goat high on a granite shelf hewn from a five thousand-foot lunge to the river, sentinels his flock. In the lofty crags, winged monarchs observe their domain. Salmon trout flash in the resting water of eddies. Elk and deer drift to the canyon bed as deep winter transforms the rim country to sifting seas of white. The river is mother to the wild. The river is sanctuary.

More than thirty years have passed since the narrative chapters of this canyon odyssey were written, and I have returned often in memory but only twice to savor it fully. In 1956, flying in our light plane up the Snake from Lewiston, my husband piloted me high over the country of Idaho's great canyons. I could only guess at the location of the long-deserted school camp high above the Snake. Impossible to identify was any place on the Salmon where I lived and taught and rode. At last I had seen that vast expanse of torrents and canyons in its entirety, but the feel of it was gone. High flight had revealed an awesome panorama, but kinship with it was lost.

Back at my news desk, I ground out a feature story on the early struggle for water along the Snake, with memory my chief incentive.

In 1970, disturbed by rumors of "development" on the Salmon and more dams on the Snake, I returned—this time, the hard way. The Snake had been maimed, but its deep canyon was undamaged. Still ferocious, the Salmon ran clear and deep. The sky was intensely blue with far horizons sharply etched. I tramped some of the old trails now widened by the forest service. True, there was an occasional bridge replacing the old ferries, but basically it was unchanged.

Affinity was restored. I returned to my desk and began a continuing plea to congressmen of Oregon and Idaho to fight for the protection of these great rivers and their environment.

Most of the old names are gone, irrelevant since my narrative does not identify those now departed persons but truly their images. They were vertical people, without pretense and real as the rock of their canyons. They are as constant in my affections as is the country where they lived and managed their place.

Glossary

cheat. A grassy weed

chock. A wedge or block

declivity. Descending slope

escarpments. Steep slopes separating two comparatively level surfaces resulting from erosion

fiddle-footed. Prone to wander

hame bell. Attached to collar of draft horse

heat-raddled. Confused

hobnail. Large-headed nails for studding shoe soles

jerkwater. Referring to a remote location

perdurance. Long continuance

remuda. Herd of horses

rick. A stacked pile of wood

raiment. Clothing, garments

roach. A mane trimmed so it stands straight up, crew-cut style

saddle cantle. The upward projecting rear point of a saddle

sere. Withered dry grass

squalled – To squall: A screeching noise made by the brake against the block

switchbacks. Zigzag roads made for surmounting steep hills

toque. A woman's soft, close-fitting hat without a brim

travois. A vehicle consisting of two trailing poles bearing a platform or net for the load

tricotine. A sturdy suiting woven of tightly twisted yarn into a double twill

About the Author

Katherine Wonn Harris was a credentialed teacher, woman's counselor and newspaper feature writer. She wrote "Topping Out" to describe the life and the terrain of "that great big beautiful country of the Salmon and Snake Rivers, and what is now called Hells Canyon."